P9-EFG-712

Red Rage

Brigitte Blobel
AR B.L.: 4.6
Points: 8.0

UG

BRIGITTE BLOBEL

Translated by
Rachel Ward

annick press
toronto + new york + vancouver

Text © 2007 Brigitte Blobel
English language translation © Rachel Ward, 2007

Annick Press Ltd.

Original title: *Roter Zorn* by Brigitte Blobel
© 2006 by cbj Verlag, a division of Verlagsgruppe
Random House GmbH, München, Germany.

 The publication of this work was supported by a grant from
the Goethe-Institut.

Cataloguing in Publication

Blobel, Brigitte, 1942–
Red rage / by Brigitte Blobel ; translated by Rachel Ward.

Translation of: Roter zorn.
ISBN 978-1-55451-102-0 (bound)
ISBN 978-1-55451-101-3 (pbk.)

I. Ward, Rachel, 1978– II. Title.
PZ7.B6193RE 2007   J833'.914   C2007-902554-4

Copyedited by Heather Sangster
Proofread by Melissa Edwards
Cover and interior design by Lisa Hemingway
Cover photo © Martin Walls, reprinted with permission
Printed and bound in Canada

Published in the U.S.A. by	**Distributed in Canada by**	**Distributed in the U.S.A. by**
Annick Press (U.S.) Ltd.	Firefly Books Ltd.	Firefly Books (U.S.) Inc.
	66 Leek Crescent	P.O. Box 1338
	Richmond Hill, ON	Ellicott Station
	L4B 1H1	Buffalo, NY 14205

Visit our website at **www.annickpress.com**

1

THAT NIGHT SHE'D DREAMT of blood, probably because she'd had a sudden attack of stomach cramps but was too tired to be woken up by them. Everything had been okay in the morning, though; the cramps had gone. So she'd left the box of tampons in the cupboard and been in a somewhat decent mood, turning up at school in pale jeans and her black anarchy T-shirt. For once she was on time for her first class because she'd wanted to give her homeroom teacher, Mrs. Sidler, a feeling of achievement for a change. Mrs. Sidler was always pleased if the whole class appeared because there were a few empty desks almost every day.

There were loads of reasons for skipping school, but nobody spoke about them. The students didn't talk among themselves, nor did the teachers or parents. They didn't discuss the kids' lack of interest and their frustration—or the violence and fear that had been spreading since a few gangs had formed in the school.

The gangs. Mara knew them all. She knew the girl gang too, who'd got in on the act, trying to rip off the younger kids in the way the guys had been doing for years. Only worse. Not that she spoke to them. She did her own thing, went her own way.

Brentwood School still had a good reputation in public, which was obviously all they cared about—the school board, the teachers, the parents, the local residents. That's why nobody spoke about what really went on in the school.

It was important to most parents to know how things were going at Brentwood. But there were others who simply didn't care what went on or whether their children were learning anything. Like Mara's parents.

In the area where she lived—pre-fab concrete tower blocks to the south of the city—nobody talked about studying anyway. Because nobody talked about education or jobs, never mind a career. Once, when Mara asked a guy on her street who was about her age what he wanted to do later on, he'd looked suspicious at first and then said, "Do? I'll be on welfare." That's how it was.

Her teacher, Mrs. Sidler, was one of those people who wistfully recalled that once upon a time when she was young, there had been jobs for everyone. Back then, school was somehow fun.

Sometimes it was amusing to Mara when she saw her teacher enthusiastically telling stories, explaining grammar, or taking the world apart and putting it right again. She seemed like someone from a different planet, someone who just didn't get it or who didn't see the reality of what many students came from every morning. And what they went back to in the afternoon. Mara wondered if Mrs. Sidler wanted to cling to some part of that "once upon a time" feeling because it was nicer back then.

So Mara had turned up on time, only to discover they had a substitute teacher for the first two classes because Mrs. Sidler had phoned in sick. I could have stayed in bed after all, thought Mara resentfully. She didn't get nearly enough sleep as it was. Their huge apartment block was always noisy because the walls were paper-thin. If someone used the toilet, you could hear it two floors below. Sometimes the police showed up in the night with their sirens blaring, or the baby next door screamed. Then Mara would get up again and switch on the TV. She could never turn it off before the show was over, even if she didn't care about the story. She had to know who got killed and who didn't, how the story finished. Back when she'd still read books, it was the same. If she started reading, she couldn't be happy until she got to the end.

The third period was music with Mrs. Granger. Today they were studying Mozart. The fourth was physics with Mr. Warner. Magnetic fields, the objects that attract or repel.

Mara actually found it interesting, but physics class was always noisy. Jing and Ishmael, over by the door at the front, were programming new ring tones into their cell phones, not giving a shit about Mr. Warner's reproachful looks. Gregory and Vladimir, a few rows behind them, were tipping their chairs back and scratching them across the floor. Jasmine, at the single desk by the window, was humming her favorite song to herself and beating time with a ruler. This is hell, thought Mara. There's no peace anywhere. Not at home, not here at school—it's all one noisy hell.

Then she felt the stomach cramps again. Suddenly, it had started. She could have kicked herself. Why was she wearing pale jeans when she knew that her period might come any time? Why did she always make the same mistake? It was some unwritten law—she never wore pale clothes except on days when it was the worst thing to do.

She hunkered down in her chair and pulled her head into her shoulders, feeling nothing but the pain in her belly, the regular recurring cramps. Sabrina, a girl in her class whose sister had a baby at seventeen, said they were like a weak form of contractions. Mara felt something hot and damp between her legs. Her denim jacket was hanging on the back of her chair.

The jacket had been passed down to her by Simone, her sister, but Mara had pulled off the sequins and little stars Simone had plastered all over it when she was in some romantic phase. Then she'd stubbed cigarette butts onto it and enlarged the burn holes with a lighter, got them nicely singed around the edges. Now the jacket was cool. Mara's favorite. She always wore it with the collar turned up and the sleeves pushed back. She liked to wear it with worn-out crocheted sweaters with extra-long sleeves down to her fingertips. Some people at school said that Mara looked like a homeless person. She was fine with that. She'd spent years working on getting people to hate her and to be bothered by what she wore. The only thing nobody could knock was her sneakers. They were quiet, flexible, and reliable. Mara was a good runner. So far, nobody had ever been able to catch her, whether a police officer was after her or some guy had challenged her.

The jacket was caught on the back of the chair, and Mara half turned around to yank it free, which meant she had to look at Rosa Riccione's fat face. Rosa was a fast-food junkie. She couldn't survive without a daily fix of greasy fries and double hamburgers with cheese and mayo. The worse her grades got, the more she turned to food for comfort. After she'd had to repeat grade 8, she'd steadily gained weight and gone up a size every two months. The problem for Rosa's parents, who ran a clothing alteration service, was that it's much easier to take pants in than to let them out. Their daughter's stomach had developed jiggly rings of fat, one above the belt and one below. Mara couldn't stand fat people. Not that she could stand anyone much. Rosa sat immediately behind her.

When their eyes met, Rosa's big, soft lips curled into a smile. She was one of those girls who goes through life begging for love while permanently apologizing for her very existence. Mara sneered at Rosa, wrapped her jacket around her waist, and half stood up, straddling the chair. She checked whether there was a bloodstain on the seat. It looked okay. So she stood right up, pulled the jacket down over her bum, tweaked it to make sure her crotch was covered too, and said, "Mr. Warner? Can I go to the bathroom?"

The physics teacher turned around from the board, put the chalk down on his desk, and wiped his fingers on a paper towel. "Now?" he asked, frowning. "I was just about to ask you to explain the difference between the magnetic flux intensity—"

"Mr. Warner," Mara interrupted, "it's urgent."

"—and magnetic field intensity and in what way—"

"I'm bleeding!" Mara screamed. "And if you don't let me go to the bathroom right now, there'll be a mess in here!"

There was total silence in the classroom, apart from Rosa's sudden snort of laughter. Mara could tell that people were staring at her bum as if waiting for a particularly gross horror film.

But she wasn't in the mood for drama. She had cramps, she was feeling sick, and she was furious with herself. These jeans were her only pale ones for the summer.

Mr. Warner frowned and his bushy eyebrows almost collided over his nose. He sighed.

"Go on then," he said, shaking his head, "but for God's sake come straight back! Is that clear? You know how many times your name's in the register for missing class without permission... In any case, why didn't this occur to you before?"

Mara was already in the hallway.

2

MARA SPENT THE REST of the class in the girls'
bathroom. She had used almost a whole roll of toilet
paper to make a big pad, just in case she couldn't borrow a
tampon from anyone. It was cheap gray paper. Mara had
very sensitive skin and knew that as she walked, the pad
would rub, inflame her skin, and cause a rash. That didn't
improve her mood.

She squatted on the toilet, her jeans bunched around her
shoes. She was careful to ensure her pant legs didn't touch
the dirty floor while she waited for the bell to end the class.
Somebody must have a tampon on them. Surely another girl
would help her; she'd do it for them if they asked.

She pressed her arms against her stomach as another
wave of cramps swept over her. She realized that the other
girls didn't ask her for anything. Nobody ever wanted to borrow a Kleenex, an eraser, a pen, or even a few blank sheets
of paper. Weird, thought Mara. Why the hell not?

The bell rang and a few seconds later the main door into
the bathroom flew open. The place was filled with laughter

and shouting, echoing off the high tiled walls. Then she heard the swing door open, which separated the sinks from the cubicles. She pushed her door slightly ajar, squinted through it, and groaned.

Rosa was standing there, smiling her usual shy, affection-seeking smile.

Mara resented the fact that, of all people, it was the fat lump Rosa Riccione who sought her friendship. Rosa with her soft, spongy skin and chubby hands that always felt as if she'd washed them and then forgotten to dry them. Rosa Riccione, who always started to cry if she didn't know something the teacher asked and who forgot her gym clothes on purpose, just so she didn't have to face the ridicule of the others. Rosa Riccione had got it into her head that Mara could be her guardian angel, that Mara would fight for her if she was picked on. Perhaps Rosa lay awake at night imagining Mara fighting for her, beating someone for her, stealing for her... acting as some kind of bodyguard.

Mara didn't want to consider what Rosa dreamt about in bed at night. She didn't want to have anything to do with Rosa at all, which Rosa knew perfectly well. Mara had made it ruthlessly clear. But Rosa was like a stray dog longing for friendship. She wouldn't let go. She swallowed all the insults and abuse with a grateful smile, as if you'd done her a favor. In return, she offered packages of jujubes, a chocolate bar, or both, which seemed to make her happy.

Oh yeah, they'd make a great pair: fat Rosa and stick-thin Mara. Rosa had masses of flowing red curls and Mara had long, jet-black hair. Rosa's T-shirts were the size of a two-man tent, while sinewy Mara could get away with wearing tight-fitting clothes.

Rosa had been waiting patiently for a chance to be Mara's friend. Today she got one. A good one. Mara needed something desperately, and she, Rosa, had it. A saintly smile hovered on her face as she raised her hand and held out a small box of tampons. "You need these, don't you?"

And Mara, peering around the door, saw Rosa take a step toward her with her X-shaped tree-trunk legs and thought, No! Why you? But she knew she had no choice.

Rosa stopped in front of the door and carefully pushed it a fraction wider. She stared at the jeans around Mara's feet and her underwear, which were stained with blood. "That's happened to me before," she said sympathetically.

Mara frowned at the girl. She stretched out her hand. "Give them here!" she growled.

"I always use the super ones," said Rosa, handing her the box. "The others are too small."

Of course they are, you fat cow, thought Mara. She glared at Rosa coldly, but Rosa smiled back.

"I'm glad to help," Rosa said.

Mara pulled a face and kicked the door so she couldn't see Rosa's fat body. Mara heard her leave.

The next cramp came and Mara nearly groaned aloud in pain, but she gritted her teeth, shut her eyes, and waited for it to pass. The most important thing in life was to look cool, always, all the time, whatever happened.

Two minutes later she was standing by one of the sinks. Three grade 7 girls swapping T-shirts looked at her nervously.

Mara needed to wash her underwear and she didn't want anybody to see her. "Can't you do that somewhere else?" she snarled.

The girls just nodded, pushed and shoved their way past her, and disappeared through the door. If Mara had felt better, she'd have smiled at that.

She looked in the mirror.

It was good to know that the others respected her. It might not be much to get a few kids from grade 7 to obey her, but you had to start somewhere. You could never let your guard down, even in grade 9.

Mara had already started a fight with Iris, a pretty whacked-out girl who everyone knew was on crack. She had caught Iris rummaging around in her school bag, probably looking for something she could sell. Afterward, Mara had expected to be confronted by Iris and her clique from the Devils, a club downtown. She thought the guys would be waiting to beat her up on the way home from school. But nothing had happened. Iris came back to school after a while, but since then she'd avoided Mara. That had got around, which was the idea.

Mara herself hadn't wasted her breath on it. She didn't boast about what she did. Stuff just happened.

Iris hadn't stolen anything from her because she'd been caught. But she still needed to be taught a lesson. It had to be clear that nobody, nobody, touched Mara's stuff.

She'd grabbed Iris and punched her once in the stomach. Iris fell hard to the ground. Mara went through her pockets and rolled up the five-dollar bill she'd found and burned it with a match before Iris's eyes. Iris had looked like a zombie, and was too terrified to make a sound. That was a few months ago, and thinking about it now made Mara smile. Her reflection in the bathroom mirror copied her.

She washed her panties, ran her face under the cold water, then headed out into the hallway and down the stairs.

It was a hot day. Kids were out on the school grounds, a spacious area dominated by two mighty chestnut trees. The soccer field, the north end in the shade, was crowded. Younger kids hung around the fence, while the older ones were in groups, acting cool. It looked peaceful, almost cheerful.

A few tentative guitar chords sounded from the music room as she walked down the pathway that led to the second school grounds. Mara heard sparrows chirping in the trees. She liked the old trees. There were white flowers on a few elder bushes nearby, smelling of vanilla. Here, in the other outdoor area, stood a group of grade 9 students who were part of the favorite class of every teacher at Brentwood: the nerds, model students, reading and volleyball champions. They were the class Mara hated most, because almost all of them reminded her of the things she didn't have.

Nobody could explain how the students from so-called better families happened to be in this one class. People who were driven to school by their parents, who wore designer clothes, and could be seen in coffee shops drinking latte macchiato; people who went everywhere together, like conspirators who had sworn to take on the rest of the world.

Mara was in the parallel class, the one with the bad reputation, the "problem class." And she had the worst reputation of the lot, which suited her fine.

But on this early June day, she still felt bad as she stood watching them. She imagined letting off a stink bomb unnoticed in the middle of the group, but that didn't stop the fury she could feel slowly rising inside her. As usual, it was something trivial that bothered her. Soon her pulse was racing and her throat was dry.

Even before the bell signaled the start of the next class, she was back in her classroom, stuffing her things into her backpack. By the time the hard-working students were streaming back into their classrooms, she'd left the school.

3

ON THE BUS ON the way home, Mara thought about the physics lesson, and about Mr. Warner. She liked him and his class, even if they'd clashed with each other a bit today. She was finding that physics had a lot in common with her life and her character. At least that was the feeling Mr. Warner had managed to give her—that everything he spoke about and taught had to do with her personally.

Electricity, for example: she had plenty of experience with that. She just had to think about the carpet in the living room at home and how often she got a shock when she walked across it in tights. Or magnetism, in all its forms. The force of attraction was her favorite subject. There were so many people who were very attractive and others who repelled everything. Like her. There must be something about her magnetic field, or the material she was made of—rather than magnetically attracting anything to her, she always just repelled everything, lost everything, which was fine by her.

It started with her need for physical space. She hated crowds and packed buses or commuter trains, and there was no way she would storm the malls during the sales or join the throngs of frenzied shoppers burrowing through mountains of T-shirts or blouses with the greedy eyes of the bargain hunter.

When she was on the bus, she liked to sit beside empty seats if possible. Like today.

For two stops she sat on her own, but then a guy got on who looked like a junior banker. He was wearing a suit, which he probably did every day, and he had a briefcase on his knees; it was only faux leather. His shoes were so shiny that Mara could practically see her face in them.

As he sat down, which he did ever so carefully so as not to crease his jacket, he looked at her and smiled.

Mara stared back as if she could see right through him. She had spent ages practicing that look. A look of one hundred percent total disdain: Who are you? I can't see you. You're invisible to me, less than a worm...It had the desired effect this time too: the guy squirmed in his seat, nervous and embarrassed, looked down at himself to check whether there was anything wrong. You could steal people's self-confidence just like that, with one look. These were the moments that made Mara feel really good about herself—when she could knock someone down without having to fight him or her. By willpower alone.

Mara didn't like fighting when she had her period. It affected her mood somehow. Didn't make her softer, let alone more placid, just different. She didn't trust her body at these times, didn't feel strong, so superior.

When she got the cramps for the first time at the age of eleven and a half, she'd hidden herself away for a week and wouldn't speak to anyone. Simone was still living with them then. Her sister was four years older and couldn't understand what was so bad about becoming a woman. It happened to all girls. It wasn't worth getting worked up about.

But sometime around then, Mara learned about the Greek myths at school and had to give a talk about Achilles, the son of Zeus. It had been prophesied to Achilles' mother that her son would die in the Trojan War, so she bathed the future hero in "ambrosia" (Mara loved that word), the food of the gods, and made him invulnerable. But because the mother had to hold the baby somewhere, his heel wasn't covered by the miraculous protection. It was only this one place where Achilles could be injured by an arrow or a spear — and since then Mara had imagined that her monthly period was some kind of Achilles' heel. At this time of the month, she sometimes found herself crying over nothing and she argued even more than usual with her mother. But that was all girly crap, not what she needed. She wanted to be strong and that's why she preferred to crawl away and hide on those days, only speaking if absolutely necessary and waiting for it to be over.

The guy sitting beside her on the bus suddenly jumped up. He worked his way to the exit, stumbling as the bus went around a corner. When the doors opened, he jumped off. He stood there, looking as if he didn't even know what stop he was at.

Mara was able to watch him for a while because she was facing backward. She imagined that he'd got off early just to avoid her eyes, her totally devastating look. It was a good thought.

4

THE APARTMENT WHERE MARA lived with her parents, Gary and Beth Dolan, was from a time when people urgently needed somewhere to live and nobody demanded beauty. A housing association had bought the development from the district ten years back, promising to renovate it, but the tenants soon realized that the association only wanted to raise the rents. Although the work got started, it soon ground to a halt after only two blocks had been completed, exactly one block from the building in which Mara lived. Her family's apartment had four tiny rooms, a bathroom with moldy patches on the ceiling, a toilet that didn't flush properly, no plug for the bathtub, a rusty mirror, brown tiles in the kitchen—all in what had once passed for style. Mara thought it was the ugliest place she'd ever seen.

There were tower blocks as far as the eye could see, streets on a grid, bus stops, asphalt parking lots, knee-high stinging nettles around the clotheslines, and slabs upon slabs of concrete—in the summer, weeds thrived in the gaps between them. There were fenced enclosures for the garbage bins and roofed bicycle racks but no sandpits anymore. The many playgrounds had been removed, the benches demolished, and there were no trees for shade in the summer or golden colors in the fall.

The renovated blocks had ridiculous balconies that looked as if they'd been glued on. The ugly weather-beaten doors leading to the staircases had been replaced by unsuitable reinforced-glass doors, while each floor had been painted a different gaudy color. It all seemed stupid and artificial. Mara was almost proud that she still lived in a genuine crushed-concrete gray box that was just as shabby on the outside as the inside, with bent mailboxes and graffiti-covered stairwells.

She could live with the fact that the entrance was cluttered with strollers, bikes, and bundles of old newspaper and plastic garbage bags. If it blocked her way, she just climbed over it.

Her mother, on the other hand, was constantly bothered—about the smell in the stairwell, the broken window in the hallway, the fact that the lock on the main door was often broken. Why did she care? Mara often wondered. Her mother had a panic attack if she so much as left the apartment and went down the stairs. Since her accident five years ago, she'd had a total phobia of the outside and had hardly even opened a window.

When Mara came around the corner, she saw a man in blue overalls with a canister on his back standing on the pavement outside her building. He was spraying the cracks between the concrete slabs with weed killer. Next to him stood Albert Droste, a Kleenex pressed to his mouth. Droste was the caretaker for a group of apartment blocks, employed by the housing association. He was a demigod, and all the tenants had to tremble before him.

He always wore pants one size too small and an expensive brown leather bomber jacket. In winter, the jacket was lined with fur; in summer, you could see the yellow silk lining because—like his shirt—he never did the jacket up. You could also see his gold chain on his chest hair, which curled when he sweated. The sight of his chest hair always made Mara feel sick. He liked to act macho, jingling his many keys and sliding his mirrored sunglasses into his gelled hair.

Three or four years ago, someone from Mara's building hanged himself from the ceiling pipes in the boiler room. He'd been a friendly old man who used to work for a printing company until he'd lost his job. Long-term unemployment, they called it. The man's wife was very ill. He cared for her until he couldn't cope on his own anymore; she went into a nursing home and died. He earned a little money helping out at the supermarket, stacking shelves and stuff like that. But it wasn't enough to cover the rent. He paid, but not all of it. He was too proud to go to the welfare office: he'd worked all his life, he wasn't going to beg now.

Droste was impatient. He sent the marshal over, who took the old man's television because there was practically nothing else of value in the apartment. Now the old man had nothing left to get him through the day. The next evening, a little boy from the second floor found the body. The old man had pinned a note to his chest. It read, In heaven you don't have to pay rent.

Droste didn't say a word.

The old man's name was Lewis Mayer, and a lot of tenants still laid flowers on his grave on the anniversary of his death.

Mara had known Albert Droste for years, and he always seemed to turn up when she was out on the street. He would suck in his belly, puff out his chest, try to look like a fitness guru, and grin. She thought his grin was slimy.

"Hello, Mara," he said. "What a pleasant surprise."

Mara didn't react. She sidled past the man in overalls who continued to spray chemicals over the path.

"We're going to clean this place up properly for once," said Droste. "There won't be a single blade of grass left."

Mara said nothing. She hunted in her bag for her key.

Droste came over and stood next to her, dug in his pants pocket, and held out his master key, which fit all the buildings he supervised.

"I've got my own," said Mara.

She stuck her key in the lock, turned it, and was opening the door when Droste grabbed the handle and closed it. "I need to speak to you," he said.

Mara stared at the door, the handle, Droste's pink hand, and then raised her eyes to give him the full benefit of her loathing. She stepped backward.

"Oh yeah, what about?"

Droste smiled. He stood in front of the door with his legs apart, arms crossed over his chest, gold chain shining in the sunlight. He was wearing a yellow-and-white-striped shirt (bound to be designer) that matched the lining of his jacket.

He spent a lot of money on his clothes. And cars. He drove a sports car—not exactly the latest model, but still.

"Your parents haven't paid the rent for June either. Now they're four months overdue."

"Why are you telling me and not my parents?" Mara tried to push past him, but he was tall and well built, at least six feet if not more, and he had shoulders like a linebacker.

"I tried that," he said. "Asked them nice and friendly, like normal people. But it didn't do any good."

"I don't know anything about that," replied Mara. She wanted to get into the building, into the bathroom, into bed. She didn't want to talk to him and least of all about the rent. It made her sick that her parents were always behind. They knew that Droste hassled her about it every time he saw her. He could get the Dolan family thrown out. Anyone who went more than three months without paying rent could expect an eviction notice—and they were now four months behind. But there was always enough money to spend the day down at the bar.

"What's wrong with your father? He's still got a job, hasn't he?"

"Yeah, but the company's going bankrupt or something," Mara snarled. She hated talking with strangers about the situation at home. "They aren't paying anybody. They're always putting him off."

"Why doesn't your father quit? Get something else?"

Mara looked at him. "Like there are all these jobs up for grabs, you mean? Lying around on the streets?"

"Garbage collection," said Droste. "That's a growing market. People keep throwing stuff away and it's got to go somewhere." He grinned. "And after all the strikes in the last few years it's going to be privatized too. There are jobs there. Anyone who really looks for work can find it."

"But my father does work," snapped Mara, brandishing her key again. "Weren't you listening?"

"Can I tell you something?" Droste had dropped his guard for a second and got out of the way of the door, but now he pushed her gently aside again. "That's not the reason your father doesn't pay. He drinks every last drop of money. Sooner or later he'll be washed up, and I don't want alcoholics here. It seems he can still hold down a job, but I'll tell you something, there's no room here for people like your father who can't keep away from the bottle. And he can't expect any pity from me."

"I'll tell him," said Mara. She struggled to keep her voice level. "Will you let me through now?"

Droste grinned. And didn't budge. "In a minute," he said, "in a minute."

His eyes slid appreciatively over her anarchy T-shirt and tight jeans, over the jacket she'd tied around her waist. And then they returned to her T-shirt—to her breasts—where his eyes remained glued.

Mara punished him with her icy scorn. She raised her arms and folded them over her chest.

"And what's up with your mother?"

"What do you mean?"

"I'm only asking. I hear things from other tenants."

"What kind of things?"

Droste rolled his eyes. "She's not quite right in the head, is she?"

Mara sneaked a look around to see if there was anyone to rescue her from this situation, a neighbor who wanted to go in or out, a mail courier, anyone. The man in overalls spraying the weeds had moved on to the next building. She was alone with Droste.

Now he was silent, continuing to look at her. Mara was glad that he had stopped talking about her mother. But his voice changed, something suggestive, slimy, creeping into his tone. It made her skin crawl.

"You know, you could solve the problem of the rent quite easily, Marey-babes, honey."

"My name's Mara."

"Okay, I know. You always take your name so seriously." His smile was almost fatherly, as if she were a silly little kid. Rage was stirring inside Mara again. She noticed she'd begun to tremble. That wasn't good—if she wasn't careful, there'd be problems here in a minute. She mustn't lose control.

"You're lucky I like you so much," drawled Droste. He stretched out his hand and laid it lightly on the top of her arm. Mara didn't react. She let him, but her stare became even icier.

She had developed big breasts when she was eleven. Apart from that, her body was somewhat boyish, slim with a slender waist. She couldn't understand how she could have such big boobs when her mother's were so small.

Since then, she'd tried to hide them, but it was difficult. She usually wore very tight tank tops under her T-shirts or sweatshirts to flatten her chest.

Once, she'd been to see a female doctor and finally got the courage to ask her about her breasts. But the doctor had just smiled and said her boobs were nice. Other girls would be glad to have a figure like hers.

Droste's hand was still on her arm. His voice was quiet. "You see, if I didn't…like you so much"—he grinned—"you'd have been thrown out long ago. I hope you know that."

"I've got to go." Mara shook him off.

He looked at her breasts again. "You'll be old enough soon," he said, finally stepping to the side and letting her past.

5

THE MAIL WAS STILL in the mailbox, but that didn't prove that her parents were out. They didn't notice the mail. There were only ever bills and reminders anyway. And since the beginning of the month, they'd been living in fear that there would be a letter from the housing association.

Now and again, there was a postcard from Mara's sister. Then her mother would laugh and her eyes would shine as she read out the message. Simone sent postcards so the family knew she was still alive. They'd had to make do with whatever details about her new life she could fit on a postcard—practically nothing. She never included a return address, so Mara had no idea where Simone lived. Sometimes she suspected her sister kept it that way so that the three of them wouldn't turn up on her doorstep one day with the TV, corner sofa, and two suitcases because they had nowhere else to live anymore. If Simone ever phoned, Mara always asked, "Where are you these days?"

Then Simone would laugh and become vague. She was sharing an apartment but was about to move; she was planning to move in with a colleague … Everything was always uncertain and fluid. Simone had said good-bye to her family. Mara couldn't hope for any help from Simone if the situation with the apartment got serious or if there was really no future for her father's company.

Simone had left home at eighteen. She had realized — and said so in so many words — that her family and everything about it could only ruin her life, her future prospects, her job — absolutely everything. She'd been promised a job in a shoe store downtown, and when she found out that she hadn't got it, and that she couldn't get any other job either, Simone knew what the problem was. She had been born into a family of losers, living in a loser area. "Nobody wants us, we're losers," she told Mara once. "But I don't want to be a loser, Mara, you know?" she'd added, and Mara had nodded.

But Mara hadn't really understood. She didn't feel like a loser. She was strong!

On a rainy day last April, without warning, Simone had packed her bags, taken the 71 bus to the commuter station, and was gone. Without letting Mara in on it, without saying good-bye.

When Mara came home from school, her parents had been sitting on the sofa, a whisky bottle in front of her father, her mother's face all red from crying. They were both silent and looked helpless. There were no posters of pop stars left in Simone's bedroom, no photos of her as a pirate queen at Halloween or in a flamenco dress for the school concert. Her closet was empty, and she had taken her stereo too. When Mara dialed Simone's cell phone, she heard, "This number is currently unavailable. Please try later." But the number stayed unavailable, no matter when Mara phoned. At some point it stopped working altogether. Simone had got a new one.

Her sister did come home once, in December, but only to explain that she wouldn't be around for Christmas. Her boyfriend was with her; his name was Brian and he had an old beat-up red vw. They brought two bottles of champagne for her parents, and Simone and Brian watched as the first bottle was opened and emptied. When her father opened the second one, Simone elbowed Brian in the ribs and muttered, "Come on, we'd better go."

The foam from the champagne had run over their father's hands and onto the table and the new Christmas tablecloth. Their mother groaned, and Mara didn't known whether it was because of the tablecloth or because Simone was leaving again. By the time she came back with a dishcloth, sister and boyfriend were down in the car and Mara could only see the taillights through the curtains.

6

THE MAIL WAS THE usual junk. The elevator had been broken for a week, so no change there either. The only difference was that the graffiti on the outside elevator door had just been removed. Mara climbed the stairs to the fifth floor amid the biting, eye-watering stench of the cleaning fluid.

Outside her apartment door sat a garbage bag. A see-through plastic bag, tied at the top, in which coffee grounds were mixed with cigarette ash, banana skins, and moldy sausage. There were other things that Mara didn't want to think about, such as all the empty bottles of pills. Pills were her mother's comfort food; she took them like other people ate chocolate — to make her feel better — to help her through the day, as she put it.

Mara stared at the garbage bag. Could that mean that her mother had cleaned up for the first time in weeks? Her mother kept talking about it, but nothing ever got done. Or was her father supposed to take the garbage downstairs and had forgotten it again? He forgot things like that on principle; he maintained that it wasn't part of the responsibilities of a breadwinner. He called himself the "breadwinner," although he didn't provide for them — not properly, anyway. But he thought that nothing more should be asked of him, seeing as he went out to work.

Next door lived the Vrabecs, a Czech couple who spoke broken English. They'd turned up sometime last year with a few boxes and mattresses, and then Mr. Vrabec had had new locks installed on the apartment door, three locks for one door — as if they expected to be attacked any second.

Mrs. Vrabec had been heavily pregnant when they moved in, but since then, Mara had hardly ever seen the baby in the flesh. Sometimes she heard it cry, especially at night because her room shared a wall with their apartment. The Vrabecs didn't have a stroller either. And as the apartment didn't have a balcony, Mara wondered whether the baby ever got any fresh air.

She sometimes worried about that baby, particularly because there were always grim stories about neglected children on the news. Mara was totally unsentimental, but she got tears in her eyes over reports like that, about children nobody cared for. If she saw reports like that on TV, she always went into her room or the bathroom. She didn't want her parents to see her tears. They had never seen Mara cry, at least not as far back as she could remember.

There was an unpleasant smell coming from the bag. Mara turned away. If she didn't take the garbage downstairs, Mrs. Gray from across the hall would be certain to ring the bell and threaten that her Rottweiler, Ringo, would rip the bag to shreds. Mrs. Gray was always using her dog to threaten people. Once, when Ringo had needed a walk early in the morning, Mrs. Gray had stumbled over Mara's father. He'd been to the bar and not made it all the way back to the apartment. The elevator hadn't been working again, so he'd curled up in his winter coat on the landing between the third and fourth floors to sleep it off—until Ringo started pulling at his sleeve, baring his sharp teeth, and growling dangerously.

Mara didn't take the garbage bag downstairs now. If she did, she might bump into Droste again, and she couldn't take his face or his sickening harassment more than once a day.

She unlocked and opened the apartment door.

In the hallway stood a plastic basket full of dirty laundry, a mangled box of detergent, and an empty bottle of fabric softener. Next to it was the vacuum, the cord all over the place and the nozzle twisted. Mara teetered over the mess. The whole apartment stank of smoke.

Beth, her mother, was lying on the sofa, her hands still in the rubber gloves (she really had cleaned something in the apartment), staring at the TV screen with her right eye and holding the left one shut. These days she couldn't always see with both eyes at once. That's what she said, anyway. She was as pale as ever, her hair lay greasy and lank around her face, and she was wearing a worn-out tracksuit. Her bare feet, with chipped red polish on her toes, peeped out from under a blanket; a cigarette glowed in the ashtray on the table.

"Hello," said Mara from the doorway. "Albert Droste's downstairs. He wants the rent."

Her mother jerked upright. "God, you made me jump! Can't you make yourself heard when you come into the apartment?" Mara shrugged and turned away. She shut herself into the bathroom.

Whenever she came home, Mara always went into the bathroom straight away. It was—apart from her own room—the only room in the house that could be locked. Mara had put a chain on her own door too. Even though her parents could go into her room when she wasn't there, at least she could hide when she wanted some peace.

She undressed. The weed killer had left gray splashes on her jeans. They stank. She threw her dirty clothes into the empty hamper and got in the shower. After cleaning up, she dried off and wrapped herself in a towel.

When she opened the bathroom door, her mother was standing in front of her, a coffee mug in one rubber-gloved hand, a fresh cigarette, ready to drop its ash any second, in the other.

"Why are you back so early?" Beth asked. "Shouldn't you be at school?"

"I've got my period!" Mara pushed past her. The dirty laundry was still sitting in the middle of the hallway. She kicked the basket aside with her bare foot. Her mother followed her. "There's no milk in the house and nothing for lunch," she called.

"I'm not hungry," said Mara. She slammed her bedroom door and was about to put on the chain, but sometimes her mother had unbelievably fast reactions and she was already halfway in the room.

Mara threw herself onto her unmade bed. "What d'you want?" she asked.

"If you go to the mall," said her mother, "can you pop into the drugstore? And your father's jacket is still at the cleaners. He didn't pick it up because the ticket's missing."

"Why don't you go?" Mara said, "Go yourself, for once. Take a step outside the front door by yourself for a change. You look like... like... like a corpse. And watch out for the ash!" But at that precise moment it fell onto the carpet.

Mara saw, without really looking, that her mother's chin had begun to quiver as she clung on to the doorframe, still wearing the pathetic rubber gloves.

"You know I can't go out," she whispered.

"I don't know anything about that," said Mara.

"I can't do it." Her mother's eyes were wet already. "It's no good. I've tried, this morning, I wanted to take the garbage out—"

"Really?" asked Mara, unmoved. "And?"

"I really wanted to. Look." She gestured down at herself, at the tracksuit. "I even got dressed."

That's true, thought Mara, normally you're still wandering around in your nightie until lunchtime. Those crappy nighties that used to belong to her grandmother. Mara's Grandma had been cared for at home, nursed to death, as people "jokingly" said. Now her mother was "wearing out," as Beth called it, all the nighties Grandma had owned and were still too good to throw away.

Mara couldn't eat when her mother sat at the table in one of those nighties. Grandma had been bedridden after she'd broken her hip, and Beth had given up her job as a cook to care for her. She got a weekend job, cleaning two medical offices—for a dentist and an ear, nose, and throat specialist. That was when they began never to have enough money. And when Mara and Simone often had to look after Grandma. Gary, their father, never did. He claimed that as a man who brought home the bacon, he didn't have to bother with all that. Sometimes he did sit by Grandma's bed with a glass of whisky and boast about what a great guy he was. He knew that the old woman had always taken him for a loser, but now she couldn't avoid him anymore, she had to listen to his boasting and how lucky her daughter was to have met such a brilliant man.

It was hard then, and when Grandma died, Mara thought it would go back to normal—her mother would return to work so they wouldn't have to count every last cent. But they had to pay for the funeral and the gravestone, and a short time later her mother had her accident. She had walked in front of a bus and got a head injury. Soon after that, she changed. She was suddenly afraid of everything: the buses, the squealing cars, dogs running between her legs, the looks of people coming toward her, the noise and stink of the city, even the smoke rising from the chimneys. Sometimes, on clear frosty days, she was afraid of white clouds floating across the sky.

Mara thought that her mother should see a psychiatrist, but Beth rejected any treatment, maintaining that nobody could help her anyway, least of all a "shrink." And even if she wasn't very well, she certainly wasn't mad. She'd rather keep taking her pills to fight the fear—unfortunately, they just didn't seem to help.

Beth stayed in the doorway as Mara got dressed. Mara's bare feet stepped in the fallen ash.

"I need to polish my nails again," Beth said, looking at her toes.

Mara said nothing. Her mother sighed.

"How was school?"

"Same as usual," muttered Mara

"When I was your age"—Beth suddenly threw back her head and laughed—"I liked school. I always wanted to learn, I wanted to be a—"

"Pediatrician one day, I know!" groaned Mara. "Shame you didn't get any decent qualifications."

"And do you know why? Because your grandfather, who spent his whole life working on an assembly line, wouldn't understand..."

"Mom! Let me past, okay? Where's the money? Where's the shopping list?"

"Oh yes, honey! I don't know what's the matter with me! What else do we need, other than milk?" Mara stood in the hallway next to the laundry basket. She stared at her mother. She was about to lose it. "Can't you do anything right?" she yelled. Her mother's chin trembled as she opened her eyes wide and pressed her rubber hands to her ears.

"It gives me a headache when you shout like that," she whimpered, shutting her eyes and pulling a tortured face. "I do my best. I got the washing..."

Mara went into the kitchen, grabbed the notepad and pencil, slammed them down on the table, and threw herself onto a stool.

The breakfast dishes, still smeared with dried jam, sat on the counter next to a yogurt container with a cold cigarette in it. The container was half full. The artificial strawberry smell hung around the kitchen, and piles of dirty pots and pans stood high in the sink.

Mara picked up the yogurt container with her fingertips, opened the garbage pail, saw that the bag hadn't been replaced, and put the container back on the table.

Her mother sat down next to her. "Keep your fingers crossed for Dad today," she said. She stared at her hands, noticing she was still wearing the rubber gloves, and stubbed her cigarette out next to the other one in the yogurt container. She took off the gloves, slowly and thoughtfully, almost with the elegance of a diva in a film, peeling beautiful leather gloves from her beautiful white hands. She carefully laid the gloves on top of each other.

"Why should I cross my fingers for him?" asked Mara.

"There's a meeting for everyone today. At the company office. The staff are finally going to stand up for themselves. Demand their wages." She smiled. "And then Dad can pay the rent. That's most urgent. First the rent, then the telephone, and then all the rest. Will you get cigarettes too? That was my last pack."

"I need money first," said Mara.

Beth stood up and disappeared into the bedroom. Mara could hear her opening and closing drawers, then she came back. She held out a twenty-dollar bill. "That will have to do," she said, "for everything. That's all there is in the apartment. I asked your father to stop at an ATM and get some out . . ."

Mara stared at her mother. Didn't she know that the account had been closed for ages now? She herself had heard her father having a fit about it.

"Does Dad need the jacket back from the cleaners that badly?" she asked resignedly as she stood up. "Otherwise there won't be enough. And couldn't you try to cut down?"

Beth stretched out her hands and grabbed Mara as she moved to go past her, holding her daughter tight. "Come on, give your mom a kiss," she whispered and looked at her almost as pleadingly as Rosa Riccione. "I'm a regular water-works today, I keep crying. I don't know... my whole life... I keep thinking about Grandma, her last weeks... And I can't stop thinking about your sister. Why Simone never gets in touch. Do you think she's forgotten us?"

"No idea." Mara pulled away. She couldn't kiss her mother. It was far too late for that sort of thing. They should have started years ago, when she was little. When she might have longed for tenderness. But tenderness had never been a matter of course in Mara's family. They were all afraid to be touched by other people. If they passed in the narrow hallway, they pulled in their stomachs and flattened their arms against their sides so as not to touch by mistake.

7

As Mara hauled the garbage bag out into the stairwell, she suddenly heard a noise, a hollow thud, and then a groan. A deep sigh from the very soul.

She dropped the bag and ran down the stairs to the next landing. Her father was lying there on his side. His hand was gripping the railing banisters, his face was pressed up against it, totally out of shape. He looked bright red—with all the little burst veins and his fat nose, which was a much deeper shade of red. Her father drank and had high blood pressure. "The doctors are amazed I'm still alive," he'd said once. Mara could distinctly remember him coming back from the appointment: it had been a medical, arranged by the company. He had laughed. "They're amazed I'm still alive!"

Now he looked as if he wouldn't be alive for long. His eyes were unfocused, saliva was trickling out of his open mouth, and he was groaning. Mara thought about Mrs. Gray's Rottweiler.

"Dad!" she yelled. "Stand up!" She knelt down next to

him and tried to loosen the hand clamped to the railing. "Shit! Hey! Dad, come on!"

Her father groaned and turned on his side again, so his face was pressed even farther between the bars of the railing. Mara was afraid he'd get his head through there and then be stuck as if in a vise.

"Dad, be careful!" She didn't know what to do.

He turned away and pulled a face.

It was a hideous grimace, but Mara had often seen her father drunk and knew that it was meant to be a smile.

"Mara..." mumbled her father, "it's over... you know... unemp... I'm... all over..." He raised his legs as if he wanted to stand up, but couldn't get his balance and slipped down two steps.

Mara raced back to the apartment. "Mom!" she called. "Come here, quick!"

Beth was lying on the sofa again. She sat up in shock. "What's wrong?" she asked, staring at Mara.

"Come on! Mom! Dad's down there!" She was out on the stairs again.

Her mother came out of the apartment, into the stairwell, and leaned over the railing. "Oh God," she groaned. "Oh no!" And drew back.

Mara tried to support her father as he pulled himself up laboriously against the bars. He gasped, causing a yellowish liquid to flow out of his mouth onto his jacket, shirt, and pants.

She put his arm around her shoulders, used all her strength and strained to lift him. He smelled of cheap brandy. That was the quickest way to get drunk.

Her father was more than twice her weight. He hung on her like a heavy, wet sack. Mara knew she couldn't drag him up the stairs, but she also knew that there was no other way.

"Mom!"

Beth came a few steps toward them, stretched out her trembling arms, and waited.

"Help me!" panted Mara.

Her father blinked. Perhaps he could see his wife up there on the stairs. Or perhaps not.

"That'll do, honey," he mumbled. "I want to . . . lie down . . . f'ra bit . . ."

Then suddenly Mara's mother opened her mouth and shouted, "No! Gary! You can do it!"

He stared at her. "Beth?" he asked, frowning. Suddenly he almost seemed sober. "You're . . . outside . . . out of the apartment?"

"Yes!" she shouted. "Can't you see?"

Then he pressed his lips together and nodded. He leaned even more heavily on Mara; all her ribs hurt from the weight.

Beth came down another two stairs. She grabbed his jacket and pulled on it, climbing backward up the stairs again. Then the neighbors' door opened. Mrs. Vrabec stuck her head out. Her blouse was undone and the baby was nuzzling at her breast.

"What is happening?" she asked in shock.

"Nothing!" cried Mara's mother. "Nothing! Go away! We can manage!"

Mrs. Vrabec rolled her eyes and closed the door again.

With all their strength, they pulled, dragged, and pushed the drunken toolmaker, Gary Dolan, forty-four, married, two daughters, back into the apartment and quickly closed the door.

When Mara's father realized that he was at home, rescued, so to speak, safe from other people's eyes, he was so relieved he lurched into the kitchen by himself and threw up his lunch into the sink, over the pots and pans.

8

MARA RAN THROUGH THE pedestrian tunnel, straight through the commuter station hall, bumped into travelers, knocked over bags, not reacting when people yelled after her. She ran past the information boards, the hot-dog sellers, the Starbucks, the bakery, the newspaper stand, and swerved around the information kiosks besieged by travelers with mountains of suitcases. She rounded a silver snake of luggage trolleys being shunted around by a worker with a forklift, almost fell over a homeless man rolled up in his dirty sleeping bag, and only just avoided a guide dog and a young man holding its harness. Mara ran as if her life depended on it.

She heard nothing, not the conductors' whistles, not the rumble of the commuter train, not the startled cry of the blind man, nor the public service announcements. All she could hear was her own heart thumping, hammering against her ribs: Let me out! I've got to get out of here, I don't want to be in this body anymore. Let me out right now...

She kept running like a machine, like clockwork, with long strides, farther and farther, between deserted factories and warehouses, jumping over potholes and puddles, her ears humming, a roaring behind her eyes. She didn't look to the left or right. She was waiting for the moment when her body would give her a signal: It's all right. Relax. Stop.

When she thought she could hear the signal, she was a long way from the commuter station. And the area she found herself in was as deserted as the moon. Suddenly it was harder to breathe. Rusty smoke curled from a low factory chimney, burning her eyes and biting into her lungs if she took a deep breath.

What had happened? A chunk was missing from her memory.

Mara pressed her hand to her mouth and slowly turned around full circle. She had no idea where she was. This was happening more and more often, the pressure inside her got too much, something in her brain suddenly clicked and she ran as if possessed, as if she wanted to get away from herself. And then, an hour or two later, she came to herself again in some other part of the city, in another outlying district. It was familiar, but it always finished her off. Made her a stranger to herself. She hadn't noticed that she'd been crying. Now it was as if she was seeing the world through a filthy windscreen with smeary raindrops running down it.

Not far away she could see a security hut with a barrier and a truck stopped next to it. The side of the truck read, SILVERMAN TRANSPORT. She watched as the guard came out of the hut, spoke to the driver, and the barrier went up. The truck drove through. The guard went back into his hut without a glance in her direction. Then somebody spoke, right next to her ear, in a wheezy whisper, "Have you got the stuff?"

She whirled round, narrowed her eyes. A guy was standing behind her, a junkie, thin as a rake with an emaciated face and deep dark circles under his eyes. He was wearing worn-out jeans and a hooded top. As he stretched his shaking hands out toward her, Mara saw the bruises on his lower arms. He smiled a crooked smile. His canine teeth were missing. That made him lisp when he spoke. He could be sixteen, could be twenty, but he could just as well have been thirty. He looked completely wasted.

"Wait." The guy slowly dug his fingers—you could see each of the tiny bones under his thin skin—into his jeans pocket. He emerged with a dirty rag, endlessly folded. As he unfolded it, Mara realized that it was a twenty-dollar bill.

"That enough?" the guy asked. "Can I have the stuff? Man, I've been waiting since first thing. Why're you so late? Don't you know how shit I am without the stuff? My whole body's shaking!" He held the money out to Mara. "Take it!"

Mara slapped his outstretched hand. So hard she hurt herself. "I haven't got anything!" she shouted. "Shit! Leave me alone! Fuck off!"

She looked around more closely. She was in a paved yard, surrounded by piles of containers. She could see a digger and two trucks and could hear a car engine starting up. Quite a powerful motor, judging by the rich sound. Mara had a weakness for fast cars with powerful engines. Good getaway cars. You could get across the country in one. The junkie swore. He bent down to pick up the money. He grabbed at it four times, his hands nervous, his movements uncertain.

"Rickie sent you, right?" He tried to focus his eyes on her but couldn't even manage that. "Or aren't you from Rickie?"

"No, for God's sake! I'm not from Rickie!" She pushed him away. She wanted to disappear. At once. Get back. Somehow get back to the tracks, the warehouses, past the rails the cranes ran on, through the yard behind the commuter station, then through the station, the pedestrian tunnel, and back to life. Wasn't she supposed to be shopping? Or something?

Suddenly, like lightning, she remembered what had just happened at home. Her father had no job. Her mother in fits of tears. Total chaos.

The junkie started to sway, then caught himself, and fell against her, sliding gently down her. He fell without a sound, clasping onto her legs. It made her want to puke. That's a human being, thought Mara in disgust.

She bent down, grabbed him by his hair, and used her other hand to stick her fingers in his eyes until he groaned. Then she let him go.

She picked up the money, which the guy had dropped again, and laid it on his face. "I haven't got any stuff," she said quietly into his ear. "Got that?"

As she left, she looked back once more. The junkie had sat up. And the security guard had come out of his hut with a German shepherd on a short leash. When she finally saw the factories looming up in front of her, she took a shortcut through one of the open warehouses.

Half an hour later, Mara was pushing a shopping cart through the aisles of a supermarket. She was totally relaxed again, almost cheerful. Her breathing had calmed and her pulse was normal. The humming had gone from her ears, and the roaring in her head had stopped. Because she felt so good, she let an assistant, a young Muslim girl wearing a headscarf, recommend the tastiest pasta sauce.

9

"**H**EY! HURRY UP!" ROSA called to her when Mara appeared in the hallway outside their classroom the next morning. "Mrs. Sidler wants to talk to you!"

Mara stopped as if rooted to the ground. She stared at Rosa, who was wearing her most hideous pants that day—green corduroy hipsters, with her rolls of flab bulging over her T-shirt.

But Rosa was smiling, she had something to do and that made her happy. Mrs. Sidler had said to her, Rosa Riccione, "If you see Mara, tell her to come and see me. I'll be in the staff room."

"Now? Before classes?" Rosa had asked in surprise.

"Yes, if Mara honors us with her presence for first period, which I very much hope she will." She'd laughed and added, "She's managed that a few times recently, hasn't she?"

Rosa had met the teacher at the school gate. Now she'd been waiting for more than ten minutes to pass the message on to Mara.

Mara just nodded. She didn't say thank you, and Rosa wasn't expecting her to.

As Mara headed back down the hallway, Rosa shuffled enthusiastically along beside her. "I don't know what she wants you for. No idea," she babbled. "I've been imagining all kinds of things. Do you think it's about your grades?"

Of course it's about my grades, thought Mara. She was on track to fail three subjects, and only had the grades to make up for two of them.

She was particularly annoyed about French. She thought an F in French was unfair. Oscar Benedict was famous for giving unfair marks.

Mara didn't think she was bad. She had a good accent. She'd even been told once that she was good at languages. She could speak at least a dozen words of Spanish with Miguel. The others couldn't give a shit about stuff like that. But she made grammatical mistakes in French. And she never laughed at Mr. Benedict's pathetic jokes. That was the real problem: the teacher, mid-forties, wanted to be popular with the students and acted young, relaxed, and witty. But somehow it didn't work. It seemed put on, insincere, kind of phoney. But nobody let on about it — apart from her. She refused to laugh at his jokes; just looked through him coldly.

And now Mrs. Sidler was going to tell her that she'd have to repeat the year. For the second time. It sucked. It was... hell. More than she could deal with today.

If Rosa Riccione hadn't been with her, she'd have been out of the door by now.

She hadn't slept well the night before. All of yesterday could be wiped out; the whole day from morning to night had been pure torture. She hadn't wanted to hang around at home after what had happened there, and then she'd remembered the junkie. She'd felt better after that, but really the guy was just another poor loser.

She'd dumped the shopping outside the apartment door, rung the bell, and taken off again. She'd wandered around the city for hours until she began to feel hungry. Suddenly she was so ravenous her belly hurt. It felt as if the walls of her stomach were being eaten from within. So she spent the last dollar on a bag of chips and wolfed them so greedily that she felt even worse.

She'd hung around outside the movie theater, waiting to see if anyone would leave early so she could use their ticket. Sometimes it worked, but it just wasn't her day.

As she'd walked back from the theater, past all the homeless people settling down for the night in doorways, it had begun to rain.

She'd ended up in McDonald's, sitting at an empty table and reading the paper that someone had left behind. There was no good news.

Some parents had beaten their child half to death and then just dumped it in a hospital bathroom. On the cold, bare stone floor. A day later, the child had died. And the parents were on the run. There were photos of a famous basketball player making out with a girl in a disco while his wife was in a maternity ward. A bomb had exploded on a bus in Israel injuring twenty-two children. Millions of people were starving in Sudan. And the unemployment figures here were rising...

She'd had enough.

She'd have liked a story about a girl, flat broke, who found a gym bag full of hundred-dollar bills on a park bench.

———————

SHE WAS EXHAUSTED FROM her marathon through the city, but she knew she wouldn't be able to sleep.

What had her father mumbled? Unemployed! He'd really lost his job!

When she got home after midnight, she heard her father snoring through the bedroom door. She didn't need to be quiet. Her parents slept like logs. Her mother must have been drinking this evening too. As if that would help deal with this mess.

When her alarm had gone off in the morning, she'd got dressed and downed a glass of milk. It had still been quiet in her parents' room. Her mother had never got up to see her off to school. Now her father would probably stay in bed till midday too.

On top of all that, now her homeroom teacher, Mrs. Sidler, wanted to speak to her in the staff room. And Rosa Riccione was wobbling along next to her, speculating. "Perhaps it's not even about your grades; perhaps it's about the other day."

"The other day?"

"You know—what happened on the school grounds."

Mara stopped and looked at Rosa with cold scorn. "What are you talking about?" she said, walking on.

Rosa had to hurry to keep up with her.

"When you got into a fight with the two Asian guys!" she exclaimed. "Don't tell me you've forgotten."

Mara hadn't forgotten. It had been pathetic, and she didn't want to think about it.

She'd taken them on, but they'd started it, they wanted to fight. The guys had provoked her and she'd risen to it, had let herself get annoyed. In any case, a bit of trouble in the day seemed to suit her.

She'd soon realized her mistake. The two of them didn't fight fair; they both went for her at once. (They were the kind of guys who stole cigarettes and then sold them and always seemed to have passes for dubious clubs. Bouncer types, wearing sunglasses even when it was raining.) She should have just stayed calm, stayed in control, been cool. Whatever. From the first punch she'd landed on the stomach of one of the boys, she'd known this could be tricky. He had a stomach like iron.

He hit back once, which wasn't so bad. It was as if he wanted to show her that she was just a silly little bimbo and he didn't hurt silly little bimbos. But then he'd grabbed her by her hair and dragged her a few feet across the ground. Everyone had laughed and jeered. And there were no teachers around to rescue her. He'd dragged by her hair over to the garbage cans. Then he pulled her up and shoved her head in one of the cans.

Everyone had just watched. Nobody helped her. Everyone obviously thought it was Mara's fault—that she'd started it, because she was always starting fights.

That evening, she'd felt like begging her mother to cut her hair. Dead short. Beth could do that, as she used to cut Grandma's hair and she'd been cutting Gary's hair for years—even the hair in his nostrils and ears, which Mara could never do. Never.

But, after looking at her hair in the mirror, she left it, her straight, long, black hair...

Could it really be about the trouble with the Asians as Rosa guessed?

"I didn't fight them because they're Asian," she snapped.

"I never said you did!" puffed Rosa.

"I fought them because they keep calling me a whore."

"I know," said Rosa.

"And I'm not a whore!"

"Bullshit!"

"What d'you mean bullshit? I'm not!"

"Course you're not!" Rosa tapped her forehead. "Why do they think that?"

"They live in our apartment block and saw the caretaker coming on to me once. I don't know what they've got for brains, not much apart from shit. Anyway, they totally got the wrong idea." Mara swung around so suddenly that Rosa caught her breath in shock. "Now, fuck off, okay? Or did Sidler say she wants to see us both?"

Rosa shook her head. "No, no, she didn't, only y... you, only you."

"Bye then," said Mara.

She stood outside the staff-room door, staring at it for a moment. She ran her fingers through her hair, took a deep breath, and knocked.

Exactly a second later the bell went for the start of classes and the first teachers began to stream out.

Mrs. Sidler was the last. She smiled when she saw Mara. "Oh," she exclaimed, "there you are! Perfect!" She stretched both hands out toward her.

Mara always found it disconcerting when teachers smiled on seeing her. She never got that anywhere else: her father frowned, if he noticed her at all, and her mother sighed when she came home from school. There was nobody whose face lit up on seeing her, apart from Rosa, who didn't count.

"I know you've got math now," said Mrs. Sidler. "But I've had a word with Mr. Jackson. I need to talk to you, Mara."

Mara hadn't smiled so she didn't need to become serious when Mrs. Sidler did.

"What about?" she asked. She could think of loads of things that her teacher might have wanted to talk to her about. But she didn't want to discuss any of them.

Mrs. Sidler put her arm around Mara. "Come on, we'll go into the parents' meeting room. We can get some peace in there and make a coffee."

She wants to drink coffee with me, thought Mara. Unbelievable. I don't get this woman. She wants to drink coffee with me, probably while she tells me I've been expelled. Or something equally brutal.

Mara tried to add up in her head how many classes she'd missed without permission this year. She couldn't work it out. Or how many times she'd been reported for all kinds of things. Rude answers, no answers at all, wrong answers, antisocial behavior, blind, destructive rage.

Mrs. Sidler opened the door to the meeting room. "Ugh," she exclaimed, "it stinks in here." She went over to the window, threw it open, and smiled at Mara again. "I could really do with a nice cappuccino," she said, "You too? I'll get them."

Mara stayed silent. When adults tried to get friendly with her, they came up against a brick wall. Mara always responded to friendliness with grumpy silence or defiance or — best of all — with indifference.

Teachers were her natural enemy. They wanted something from her, to put her right, to punish her. They wanted her time, her attention. Wanted hard work and enthusiasm.

Even if she was prepared to do Mrs. Sidler the favor of turning up to school on time now and then, she was still Mara, the silent. Who only answered when it suited her and only spoke when she could see the point herself.

When Mrs. Sidler spoke to her, she rarely answered. But it seemed as if her teacher had got used to that, didn't let it bother her.

"The coffee machine was a gift from a former student." Mara just nodded. "She was quite a difficult child. Talented but lazy. And cocky. Hmm, look who I'm talking to!" She looked across at her after putting a couple of coins in the machine.

Mara didn't move. She stood, her arms folded across her chest. Waiting.

Mrs. Sidler took another paper cup from the holder and put it under the nozzle. "She got her act together at some point, though. Now Marion Takahashi owns two hair salons in the city center: Hair Affair. She's got more than thirty employees, drives a convertible." Mrs. Sidler smiled. "Ruins her hair, though. You'll have a coffee, won't you?"

Mara shook her head. "I'm not thirsty." She saw the

teacher's face fall a little. She was obviously disappointed that her relaxed style wasn't getting her anywhere. But Mara wouldn't make it that easy for the teachers. Even the one she actually liked. She wasn't to think that she could get anything out of her like that.

"Sit down, this might take a while," said Mrs. Sidler.

There were two tables in the room, each with three chairs, one by the window and one in the slightly darker corner. Mara chose the darker spot. At first she sat up straight, but then she slumped, her legs outstretched, bending her toes up and down in her sneakers. Her shoes made almost-inaudible squeaking noises. It was a horrible noise actually, but that's what Mara liked about it.

"So, now we can talk." Mrs. Sidler sat opposite her, looking at Mara. The teacher was friendly, attentive, but without the smile she'd been showing until now.

Mara waited. She was starting to feel a bit uneasy and she could sense an itch between her shoulder blades. Normally she'd have scratched it, but now she forced herself to be cool and calm. She wanted to look relaxed.

"I sent your parents a letter three weeks ago, inviting them to a meeting," said Mrs. Sidler.

Mara looked out the window in silence.

"They never answered it." Mrs. Sidler stirred her cappuccino. "I offered them a choice of three times, I was here at the school on all three evenings. But they didn't turn up."

Mara still said nothing.

Mrs. Sidler sighed, took a sip, and put the cup down carefully. Paper cups spill easily.

"Did your parents get my invitation?"

Mara's eyes wandered from the window, across the sunshine-yellow walls to Mrs. Sidler's face. The teacher was in her late thirties and had big brown eyes and full lips. She wasn't thin but was still very agile. She had a weakness for ethnic jewelry and wore long chains of heavy glass beads or metal disks, shells or silver balls over her clothes (usually in her favorite colors of brown or turquoise), and she had lots of colorful rings on her fingers. When she walked, something always jingled. She loved skirts with uneven hems, asymmetric sweaters, and even her hair was asymmetrical: one side long, the other short. Her bangs almost covered her left eye. Someone had told Mara that Mrs. Sidler was blind in one eye; maybe she had a glass eye and her strange hairstyle was supposed to cover it a bit.

So Mara had often watched her, but she'd never seen any difference between the teacher's eyes and had stopped believing the rumor.

"Well?" asked Mrs. Sidler. "Did they get the letter?"

"I expect so," mumbled Mara.

"They didn't mention it to you?"

Mara shook her head. She avoided the teacher's penetrating gaze, looked out the window again, and concentrated on not blushing.

"Do your parents know your situation?"

She shrugged.

"Yes or no? Do they know that you've had more than twelve warnings for aggressive behavior? Let alone all your entries in the register for skipping classes?"

"No," muttered Mara. "They don't know."

"What's next?"

"Dunno."

"You've already repeated one year," said Mrs. Sidler, "and you know that you're in danger of not passing again."

Mara concentrated on a speck of bird shit on the left window frame.

"You know that, don't you?"

"Yeah," she said.

"Unless you come to your senses and actually start working properly, concentrating properly."

Mara found herself grinning against her will. How many times had she heard that?

Suddenly the teacher thumped the table with her fist, making the paper cup jump.

"Have the decency to wipe that superior grin off your face while we're having this conversation! And at least try to sit up properly. There are certain rules, my girl. Even for you. I'm not here for my own amusement."

Mara coughed, slid her bum back in the seat, and sat up. She frowned to make it clear she wasn't grinning.

Mrs. Sidler sighed. "You know I hate having to talk to you like this?"

Mara pressed her lips together. What was she supposed to say to that?

"But I've got no choice. Friendliness obviously has no effect on you."

She got up and went over to the machine. "The coffee needs sugar."

Mara noticed that the heels on her shoes were wobbly. She almost grinned again, but when Mrs. Sidler came back to the table, she was staring with a frown at the bird mess. Must have been a sparrow, she thought. There's nothing but sparrows round here.

"I wanted to talk to you about your work experience placement," said the teacher.

Mara relaxed for a second; so there was no new problem, no fight to explain, no complaints from any other children. That was good.

"Everyone in your class has found a place except for you. Why's that?"

She shrugged.

"What does that mean? Haven't you even tried?"

Mara looked her teacher in the eye for the first time.

"Yes or no?"

"No."

"And why not?"

"Dunno how."

Mrs. Sidler rolled her eyes. She laughed grimly. "You don't know how? What have we been talking about for the last few weeks? Could it have been exactly how to go about getting a placement? And you were present for at least some of the classes. So?"

Mara stared at the floor.

"Have you spoken to your parents about it?"

"About what?"

"The placement, of course! Can your parents get a place for you?"

"How could they do that?" growled Mara.

"Your father has a job, doesn't he?"

Mara said nothing.

"Where does he work?"

"At Global."

"And what does he do? Talking to you is like pulling teeth!"

"Toolmaker."

"Are you interested in that sort of thing?"

"Nah."

"Have you ever visited your father at work? Do you know any more about what he does?"

"I've got a pretty good idea."

"That's not the same thing as seeing and experiencing it for yourself."

"I can't go with my dad," Mara said. "The company's gone broke. They fired everyone. My father worked for three months without getting paid and then"—she gestured with her hand—"all over."

The teacher took a deep breath and sighed, twisting the rings on her fingers. Mara thought, I've finally beaten her. Teachers always go quiet when they hear about unemployment, because it takes away their argument for bothering with school. When even your parents can't find jobs . . .

"I'm sorry to hear that." Mrs. Sidler's voice was gentle. "Last time we spoke it sounded as if things were halfway okay for your family."

Mara didn't answer.

"And your mother? She still hasn't got a job? Is she . . . uh, is she any better?"

Mara shook her head. She was slightly surprised that Mrs. Sidler had remembered what she'd told her ages ago, about her mother's accident and what had happened after that.

The teacher stared ahead for a moment, then stretched her hand out flat across the table.

"I had an idea," she said in the end. "That's what I wanted to discuss with you. It's about a work experience placement for you. I'm just not sure if it's the right thing to do. It's . . . it would be"—she hesitated and looked at Mara—"an experiment. I'm putting my neck right on the chopping block for you here, you know, you're not exactly . . ." She stopped.

Mara waited. I won't ask anything, she told herself. I'll keep quiet.

It was silent in the room.

Mrs. Sidler twisted the rings on her fingers again. Then she looked up. "I've got a niece, Janine." She coughed. "She's a kindergarten teacher, just finished training and working in a private day-care center. They are financed by private sponsorship so they're always short of money. And short-staffed."

Mara knew about day-care centers like that, as her sister had briefly toyed with the idea of training as a kindergarten teacher. But it came to nothing because everybody advised her against it. There was no point, there were no jobs. She might as well go on welfare right away.

"At this place," said Mrs. Sidler, "Janine and her boss, her name's Muriel Clement, have to look after around thirty children. From eight in the morning till four in the afternoon. I spoke to her, and she would be glad if you could help them out for a few weeks."

Mara stared at her teacher. "Me, go there?"

"Yes. Why are you looking at me like that?"

"Me, little kids...?" She shook her head. "But I... I mean... I've never... If I had a little brother or sister or something..." She couldn't believe it. "Where did you get an idea like that from?"

Mrs. Sidler watched her calmly. Mara could feel her head overheating.

"Well," mused the teacher, "I thought... that could be just what you need."

"Just what I... need?"

"Yes, it could be, couldn't it? I know you find it difficult to relate to other people, but that's with people your age or adults. You like younger children, don't you?"

Mara nodded. Who didn't like little kids? You couldn't help liking little kids, she thought. They don't hurt anyone. They just shit their diapers, make a mess with their food, can't tie their shoelaces, and always want to be read stories. And always tug at you and want you to play with them or pick them up. And they scream blue murder if they get a scratch. She knew about dealing with little kids. In theory, at least.

The teacher scrutinized her. "Janine, my niece, is nice. You'll like her. Mrs. Clement, the center manager, is very competent. Of course, she has a great deal of responsibility."

Ah, thought Mara, so she's a cow. But she didn't say anything.

"I have to vouch for you," continued Mrs. Sidler. "They don't know about your problems at school. I thought you should be able to start there without any prior baggage.

I know you can pull yourself together." She looked at her penetratingly, and Mara returned her gaze.

"If you don't take the placement or any problems arise at all, you can kiss this school year good-bye," said Mrs. Sidler. "I hope you realize that. I'm almost the only member of staff at this school who still has any faith in you. Is that clear?"

Mara looked down.

"So I advise you to accept it. It's only for two weeks, but it's a huge chance for you."

She nodded but didn't say yes.

"So if you're willing to always turn up, to always be punctual and to do what you're told," the teacher stood up, her necklace jingling, "I can call Mrs. Clement and tell her you're coming. It'll start next Monday."

Mara stood up too, staring at her feet.

"Does that mean you're happy about it?" She didn't answer. She didn't want to show any feelings. But she felt strangely warm inside.

"Too bad," said Mrs. Sidler, "I had hoped you might show a positive reaction." She opened the door to leave.

So Mara said, "I'll need the address."

The teacher turned to her. Mara returned her gaze.

"Good. I'll speak to Mrs. Clement and tell her you're coming. If it's all okay, I'll give you the address tomorrow." She nodded to her.

As Mara pushed past the teacher and walked down the long hallway, she could feel her eyes on her for quite a while.

10

ROSA WAS ALMOST BURSTING with curiosity. She stared at Mara as she made her way to her seat. But Mara didn't respond. She sat down, opened her books, and tried to follow what the teacher was saying. Once, Rosa must have bent forward and poked Mara in the back with her pen, but Mara didn't turn round.

But she couldn't avoid her at break. Rosa waddled up to her in the hallway. Outside, it was pouring with rain. And the noise coming from the hall was like a hip-hop club.

"Well? What did she want? Are you in trouble?" she asked. "Was it bad?"

Mara stopped. She looked at the girl as if she was an annoying insect.

Rosa tried to smile at her, but then she retreated in shock, leaned against the wall, and stood there, her head to one side as if she was expecting a punch.

"It's none of your goddamned business what she wanted from me, okay?" Mara was right up against her, her voice dangerously quiet. Rosa's lips twitched and it looked as if she was about to cry.

"And if you don't stop following me about like some pathetic stray dog, then I'm going to lose it on you, got that?"

"Yes," whispered Rosa, shutting her eyes. Mara saw the little tears appearing on her pale lashes. She couldn't stand girls who cried in public. "And if you ever stick your crappy little pen into my ribs again, I'll stick it back, but in your eyes or some other part of your flabby anatomy, where it will really hurt," hissed Mara.

"I didn't mean to annoy you," sobbed Rosa. Her voice was trembling.

Mara grabbed Rosa by the shoulders and slammed her twice against the wall; there was almost no sound because Rosa's back was well padded. It probably didn't even hurt her.

———————

THERE WEREN'T ANY FREE seats on the bus. Mara had to stand. A crowd of baseball fans, wearing the red-and-white ball caps and jerseys of the home team, pushed their way down the aisle. They were on their way to the afternoon's game. Mara was interested in baseball but not that team. The local rivals were her favourites, because they were were winners, swept all the others away. When one of their games was on TV, Mara always sat next to her father on the sofa, pigging out on potato chips while her father swore, drank, and shouted at the screen.

Mara held tight to the strap as the bus jolted around a

corner. It was always uncomfortable here where the bus crossed the train tracks. The bus lurched. Her backpack swung into someone's stomach. She heard an "oof."

Mara looked straight into a boy's face. He had strangely iridescent eyes, and there was a tiny mole above and to the right of his top lip—it was almost heart-shaped. The guy was probably about sixteen.

"What have you got in there?" he asked, pointing at her backpack. "Rocks?"

"Something like that," muttered Mara. She slipped the heavy bag off her shoulder and put it between her feet.

When the bus stopped suddenly, the backpack tipped over and came open.

"Oh," said the boy, "I guess that's my fault, isn't it?"

Mara didn't answer, as she didn't respond to pick-up lines on principle. She bent down as well as she could and collected her things, the ruler, the set-square, the math book covered in stickers of her favorite band, a three-colored pen, and a few notebooks.

As she straightened up again, he asked, "Is math your favorite subject?"

"Do I look like it is?" snapped Mara. She sounded angrier than she'd meant to.

But he laughed. "I don't know what someone who likes math looks like. Your math book is cool. Which school do you go to?"

"Brentwood," she snarled.

"Oh," he said. "Breeding ground for criminals, as they keep telling us."

"You're full of yourself, aren't you?" retorted Mara.

He grinned and pointed toward her. "She's blushing!"

She wondered why this guy was so persistent, as most of them gave up pretty damn quick when they got one of Mara's grumpy answers. They usually turned away, shrugged, and stopped bothering with such a moody girl.

This one was different. Her answers didn't faze him. They just made him laugh. He was the sort who could just laugh off a bad mood.

When he turned away briefly to read the street signs through the window, Mara sneaked a closer look at him. He had light-brown hair, straight and chin length, and he was trying to grow sideburns—without much success as that hair was a bit darker and very curly. Boy, thought Mara, can't you see that it looks ridiculous?

He turned around sooner than she'd expected and Mara blushed again. "I'm at the Bolivar School." When she only shrugged indifferently, he added, "Taking modern languages. I'm no good at math." He laughed again.

Mara pulled a face.

The brakes squealed. There was someone in a wheelchair at the bus stop. The bus floor was slowly lowered, so the passengers were at a slant—not easy for the ones standing up. Mara was thrown slightly against the boy. He took her arm and held on to her tightly. She could smell the skin on his neck and something coming from his jacket. Licorice, she thought. He's got an open box of licorice.

The bus returned to the horizontal.

"You don't always get this bus, do you?" the boy asked as he let go.

"Depends," answered Mara evasively. "Sometimes I get an earlier one, sometimes I get a later one, depends on what classes we have."

"But usually this one on Wednesdays," he suggested.

She looked at him, narrowed her eyes. That was true, Wednesday was a long day, longer than the others. "Have you been watching me?" she asked suspiciously.

The boy laughed. "I just notice some girls. There's no law against that, is there?"

Shit, thought Mara. If I blush for a third time, I'll punch myself in the face. So she concentrated, and she didn't blush. Then she thought, He noticed me. Hmm. No, no law against it.

"In case you were wondering why I haven't introduced myself—"

"I didn't ask you," replied Mara hastily.

"Allow me. Harris, Tim. Tim Harris."

He made a comic bow. The guy seemed to be in a permanently good mood.

Mara wedged her bag more firmly between her feet because they were going around another corner, on the other side this time.

"And may I ask your name?"

"Mara."

He raised his eyebrows and looked at her.

"Hey, nice name." His voice was soft.

"Is it?" she said.

The bus stopped. A few people got out and there was more space so Tim moved away from Mara a bit.

"I get off at the next stop," he said.

Mara nodded in silence.

"Perhaps we'll see each other again," he said.

"Perhaps," she answered.

"I'll look forward to it."

She looked past him. She looked out of the back window. So he lived around here somewhere, she thought. In this nice area. With trees, big front gardens. Older townhouses. Some were a bit run down but others were renovated, gleaming white like something in a movie.

Mara came down here every day (when she wasn't skipping school) and knew the route by heart, even this road. But it seemed different today—as if she could see more than usual.

"Do you live here?" she asked, pointing out of the window.

"Just around the corner. 12 Cudworth Way. How about you?"

The bus stopped. The doors opened. Tim was already halfway through them but waiting for her answer.

"Farther on!" she called. "South of the city!"

He nodded, waved. "See you," he said, jumping onto the sidewalk.

Mara didn't look back as the bus drove on. But she had the feeling that Tim had waved again.

12 Cudworth.

She wondered where the street map was at home. It'd be interesting to know exactly where Cudworth was.

11

HER FATHER HAD OPENED the living-room curtains. He was standing at the window in a vest, his bare arms crossed over his chest, looking down at her.

She never usually looked up to the fifth floor, to their apartment. It wasn't like there was anything to see: the curtains were always closed, there was no balcony that you could go out onto, no birdcage on the windowsill, no cat sunning itself, nothing—just drawn curtains all year round.

Mara's mother was afraid of the noises from the street. She didn't like it when the people in the opposite building could look into their apartment. The sun only ever came in through those synthetic curtains, filtered, weakened; it was never properly light either in their living room or any other room. They'd got used to it.

But that day her father was standing by the open window, and if Mara had looked more closely, she might even have been able to see the tattoo on his arm from here. When she glanced up, he gave no reaction. She thought about waving to show that she'd seen him but decided against it.

It was odd that he was standing by the window in his vest. By the open window. She felt her skin crawl. She walked faster. Something was driving her on.

Mara glanced at her watch. 3:30 p.m. She tried to calm down. What could be wrong? Her father would be at home every day now. She'd have to get used to that. Perhaps he'd often be standing by the window when she came home from school; perhaps he'd persuaded her mother to leave the curtains open from now on so that he could look out. He had to do something to pass the time, as he couldn't spend the whole day in front of the TV.

She didn't look in the mailbox. She walked up the stairs, but the higher she climbed, the stronger the feeling grew—something wasn't right. She moved slower and slower, and her legs felt heavy. She had to grip the railing.

The apartment door was ajar slightly. She could smell cold smoke and cup-a-soup. There was no sound from the apartment: no jingling music, no droning radio, no chatter from the television, not even her parents arguing. It was dead quiet.

Mara cautiously pushed the door open farther with her foot. She didn't know what she was afraid of, but she was now definitely afraid. She slipped the backpack off her shoulders and took off her sneakers. The whole time she was listening attentively. There was absolutely nothing to hear.

Perhaps her father was still standing by the window. What was he doing there?

The kitchen looked the same as ever: empty beer cans on the table, the sink full of pans and dishes, an overflowing garbage bag next to the trash can with a crushed carton of apple juice sticking out of the top.

Where was her mother? Was she still asleep? It was possible; she'd soon know. Before she went into the living room, before she even said hello to her father, however, she had to know what state he was in. Recently he'd been able to hold less and less drink, yet drunk more and more. But she couldn't see anything except beer cans. No empty whisky or wine bottles.

She went into the living room. Her father was still standing by the window, in his vest, workpants, and suspenders. He'd lost weight in the last few months so he'd received the suspenders for his birthday, as a joke. They were wide and red, so as not to look too old-fashioned.

"Hello, Dad."

Her father turned around. Slowly. In super slow-mo. His face was white, but his lips were strangely blue and his eyes were wandering.

"Back already?" he asked.

She nodded. She watched him as he went from the window to the armchair, walked around the chair, and sank into it.

"Your mother's in the hospital," he said.

Mara jumped. "What?"

"I took her there. And I wanted to bring her home again, but the asshole of a doctor said she should stay in for observation. He ought to know what's wrong with her. He doesn't believe our story. What a shit. Goddamned nonsense. I mean, what is there to observe? What's that meant to mean? They're out to get me, that's what it is."

Mara cleared her throat. "What happened?" She was still standing in the doorway.

He looked at her. "What happened? Nothing. We had a fight. What's that for a doctor to get worked up about? There's disagreement in every good marriage, isn't there?"

Mara shut her eyes. She took a deep breath. She didn't want her voice to shake. "What happened?"

He looked at his hands, as big as shovels, stared at them as if he'd never seen them before.

"She fell against the cupboard," he said. "She tripped. You know how wobbly your mother is on her legs, don't you?"

Mara came into the room and saw for the first time that the glass in the cupboard door was cracked. Shattered. The splinters of glass were all over the place. And two vases were broken. The china vase with flowers on it and the red glass vase.

"Fell against the cupboard?" queried Mara.

"Yes, for God's sake! Your mother fell against the cupboard! Why do you keep repeating everything? Is there something wrong with your ears, or is your hair so long you can't hear properly?"

He lurched out of the armchair again, came toward her. And now Mara saw that he was drunker than she had thought. She could always tell by his half-closed eyelids, this strangely sleepy expression. She drew back into the hall.

He followed her. "Oho!" he yelled. "Are you afraid of me? Of your own father? Are you getting like your mother? Can't a man say anything anymore? Yes, damn it, my hand slipped. She was asking for it, understand? You know what she's like, she can drive you nuts. So you don't know what you're doing."

Mara's heart was thumping painfully; suddenly her whole chest hurt. But she held back. She looked at her father as if she could force him to stop.

"What did she do?" Mara asked.

"Do! Do!" her father shouted at her. "What did she do? What didn't she do? Does it matter? Go and ask her. But if you go, don't bother coming back, okay? You're either on my side or hers. Haven't I damn well fed you all these years? I could have spent my money on myself; then I'd have got a nice car by now. And I'd go fishing whenever I'd want and wouldn't have to prowl around in this cage." He stared at the little hall cupboard and kicked it over with one mighty blow.

"Dad!" screamed Mara. "Stop it!"

He stopped. He looked at her. "You want to tell me what to do as well now?" he snarled. "What a shit family I've ended up with! Shut up, for God's sake. Shut up!"

He stood in front of her. He was dripping with sweat; all the alcohol he had consumed that morning oozed out of his pores.

Mara was revolted, but she said nothing and waited.

"If Beth, if your mother, presses charges against me for assault"—his voice was dangerously quiet now—"then it's over, got that? All over. Then she can see how she'll cope on her own. If she reports me to the police and says I hit her, and if the police turn up here... It's over..." He looked at her threateningly. "And you keep your mouth shut too."

"Whatever," said Mara. "You've got to work that out for yourselves."

Her father nodded.

"Yes," he said. "Work it out for ourselves."

With that he turned around and lurched down the hall into the bathroom.

Mara went into her room and locked the door behind her, leaned against it. Breathing hard, motionless, she stood there for several minutes, her eyes closed.

What a mess her family was, what crap this all was. She didn't know what would happen next. She just knew that she didn't want anything to do with it, that it was her parents' duty to get some kind of grip on their lives. She had enough to do for herself. She opened her eyes.

It was good to look around her room. The walls, a window ahead, the door behind her. A space she could shut off from the world. Everything here belonged to her: the bed with an Indian throw; posters of her favorite bands and her pinboard covered in photos and stickers; her CD collection, not much admittedly, but all special (techno and heavy metal); under her bed, the lovely white shoebox in which she kept her most personal things; a desk in front of the window with a lamp that she could dim to create a really cozy atmosphere... She took a deep breath, inhaled the scent of the lavender spray she'd bought on special offer in a drugstore to combat the reek of smoke and alcohol that infested the rest of the apartment.

Yes, she had a nice room. A calm, peaceful room, her refuge, her fortress. Outside it, the front door slammed. Her father was probably going down to his bar. He'd be a while.

12

BETH CAME BACK THAT evening. She had checked herself out. She'd explained to the doctor that she suffered from dizzy spells and that was why she'd fallen against the cupboard, but the doctor hadn't believed her. He'd kept asking her questions about her marriage, but she'd stuck to her explanation.

The cut on her head had been stitched and her right shoulder was bandaged.

Mara hadn't heard her come in; she was in the middle of doing the dishes from the last few days. Suddenly her mother was standing at the kitchen door.

"Hello, sweetie," she said and grimaced, a shaky, pain-filled smile.

Mara dropped the cloth into the dishwater. She ran to her and hugged her.

Beth moaned.

"Sorry!" Mara drew back.

"It's okay, it just hurts a bit. I bruised my shoulder in the fall. Is he here?" She threw a cautious glance toward the living room across the way.

Mara shook her head.

Her mother sighed with relief. "Oh good. I was thinking," she hesitated and looked timidly at Mara. "I wanted to ask you . . . would you mind if I slept in your bedroom?"

Mara stared at her mother as if she were from another planet. "You're not serious," she said.

Beth forced another smile.

But Mara shook her head. "But that's my room! It's the only room that belongs to me! You've got the whole rest of the apartment!"

"Your room is the only one with a lock. I need to feel safe at night. Besides, what about the bathroom? And the kitchen?" asked her mother. "You use them, don't you?"

Mara couldn't believe that her mother really meant what she was saying. Couldn't she see what she was asking of her? "And what kind of a room will that leave me? Where am I supposed to hang out?"

"In the living room? On the sofa?" her mother suggested tentatively.

"And what about when Dad comes home?" yelled Mara. "You want him to sit on the edge of my bed? When he's drunk?"

Beth stroked her hair. "He won't hurt you, you know that." She looked at her daughter in desperation. "Please, just for tonight."

It was true. As long as Mara could remember, her father had only hit his wife, never the children. "I won't touch the kids," he'd always said. "My daughters are sacred to me."

When the girls were little they'd lain huddled up together in Simone's bed while their parents argued and her father got violent, but nothing had ever happened to them.

Mara wanted to help her mother—so in the end she agreed. But just for tonight.

Beth's shoulder injury meant that she couldn't undress herself, wash herself, and comb her hair. She was helpless.

Mara did all that. It was years since she'd been as close to her mother as now, but it stressed her out too, gave her a headache.

"Why did Dad do this?" she asked. "He's never... this bad..." Finally Beth was lying in bed, staring with wide eyes at Mara's pinboard, as if it was the first time she'd been in her room. As if she hadn't heard Mara's question.

"My God," she said, "all those garish posters. What do you want them for?"

"No reason," said Mara. "Are you going to answer my question?"

Beth turned to face her daughter, who was leaning against her desk, her arms crossed over her chest.

"He's just angry because he's unemployed. He thought he'd be able to... to get old with that company, work there until he retired."

"And that's why you argued?"

"We were talking about money. It's always about money when we argue."

On the pinboard was a photo of Mara and her sister at a New Year's Eve party. They were both wearing pointy, glittery paper hats and streamers were tangled around their necks and shoulders, as if they were chained down by them. They were both smiling toward the camera.

"He wants me to go out cleaning again," said her mother quietly. "But I can't, I can't do it. I can't go out."

"You've been out now," said Mara.

Beth sat up a bit. "Yes," she said, letting her head fall again. "I've been out now. In a taxi... It wasn't that far..." She shut her eyes.

Mara waited. Her mother was breathing shallowly, her eyelids fluttering.

"Do you have any idea what'll happen next?" she asked.

Beth shook her head. "I need to sleep. The doctor gave me some pills to calm me down. I'm dead tired." She turned onto her good shoulder and drew her legs up to her chest.

13

M RS. SIDLER HELD ON to Mara's arm as she tried to leave the classroom after English, the second last class of the day. Rosa had already left, which was good because Mara didn't want to see her face, and almost all the other students were already out in the hallway.

"Mara? Just a second. I want to give you the address of the day-care center," said Mrs. Sidler. "I spoke to Mrs. Clement. She'll be glad to see you if you can start on Monday."

Mara had hardly thought about the day-care center. "I don't know if I can," she hesitated.

At once her teacher's face became serious, almost cold.

"Really?"

"I don't know whether I can be away for the whole day."

"And why not?"

"My mother is ill. I ought to look after her in the afternoons at least."

"What's wrong with her, something serious?" asked Mrs. Sidler. Mara could feel her suspicion.

"She's not well."

The teacher looked her in the eyes. "You told me about your mother. I know it's difficult for you. But your life is important too, you have to realize that."

Mara said nothing.

The teacher was holding a piece of paper with the address in her hand, folding it up, rolling it up tightly, smoothing it out again. She was silent and so was Mara.

"You're not making this easy for me. You know what will happen if you turn down this placement?"

"I'm not turning it down," replied Mara, "I just can't do it."

Mrs. Sidler looked at her. "Because your mother is ill?"

"Yes," answered Mara, "exactly."

"Why can't your father look after her? If he hasn't got a job, he must be able to do that."

Oh God. Mara felt hot all of a sudden. How do I get out of this one? Should I say, It was my father who beat my mother up, so she can't do anything for herself? Should I say that?

She looked at the floor.

A younger boy stuck his head around the door. "Mrs. Sidler?" he yelled. "There's a woman looking for you. She wants to talk to you!"

The teacher raised both her hands as if to fend him off. "Not now, Toby! In a moment! You can see I'm in the middle of a conversation."

The boy looked uncertain, glanced around, then disappeared.

"So?" the teacher turned back to Mara.

Mara swallowed. She choked on the sentence. The

sentence was like a lump, getting bigger and bigger, para-lyzing her tongue.

Mrs. Sidler looked seriously at Mara while she fought with herself.

"Don't make things so hard for yourself," she murmured urgently, putting her arm around her. "Just spit it out. It'll help to talk about it."

Mara was desperate, and she hoped that it didn't show in her eyes. She felt an unbelievable fury, a hatred toward all the things she couldn't speak about. She had never talked about what went on at home, never. Her pride wouldn't allow it. But it was almost choking her.

Mrs. Sidler folded up the little slip of paper and was about to stick it back in her pocket when Mara stretched out her hand. "Give it to me, please. I'll go, I'll be there on Monday."

"Are you sure?" asked the teacher. "Quite sure?"

"Yes," she took the paper. "What time?"

"Eight o'clock. Perhaps you can look after your mother for a bit before you go."

Mara nodded.

She wanted to say thank you, but she couldn't get the words out. It was no good.

"I hope you do well at the day-care center. As I said, if you get a good report from them it can only benefit you here at school. Just working with little children might show you that your social behavior—"

Suddenly the door opened again and a woman came into the room.

"Mrs. Sidler?" she inquired. "I need to speak to you urgently. I already telephoned..." She came straight toward the two of them without even so much as a glance at Mara.

A welcome interruption. Mara shouldered her backpack. The teacher gave her a little smile as she left.

"Rosa is my daughter," said the woman. "My name is Renata Riccione..." It was Rosa's mother!

Mara fled.

But she stopped for a moment behind the closed door, listening. She heard Mrs. Sidler asking what it was about and saying that she had to get back to her class after the break.

"What I have to say," responded Mrs. Riccione, "doesn't have to take long. It's a matter of the conditions prevailing in Rosa's class. There are unbelievable things going on here!" She took a deep breath, ready to launch into an explanation.

Mara sped down the corridor, down the stairs, and was outside in seconds flat. She gave herself the rest of the day off.

14

MARA COULD HAVE GOT the next bus, the one at thirty-six minutes after the hour, or the one at six minutes to, but she sat in the bus shelter and didn't get on, first let one and then the other go by. She wanted to get the same bus as on Wednesday. It finally came.

Today there was plenty of room. No game, thought Mara. Good. No meat-head armchair athletes either, talking big and usually acting so moronically that she could hardly stand it.

She wondered what Rosa's mother was telling her teacher. She'd only been a bit rough with the girl a few times recently, but there'd always been a reason, like yesterday, when she'd constantly followed her after her conversation with the teacher. Rosa knew that Mara couldn't stand that. She could have just left her alone, and then nothing would have happened. But all the same, hardly anything worth talking about had happened. Although there was that incident two weeks ago. Had Rosa only just mentioned it?

Mara thought back. She'd bumped into that gang from grade 9, a group of girls that she wanted nothing to do with. She loathed them. Two of them were punks, Sara and Laura, with multiple piercings and dyed-black hair that they wore in little tufts, sticking out wildly from their heads. And their signature was handcuffs on their belts, not real ones, obviously, but the sort you can buy from costume stores. Mara thought it was totally pathetic. The other two, Nadine and Helena, always swaggered around like town toughs, bow-legged as cowboys. The four of them were inseparable. They always had the latest cell phones, iPods, whatever: so long as it was expensive, and looked it.

Everyone knew about them at school: where they got the cash from, how they ripped off the younger kids, stole their phones, took their clothes.

The four girls shoplifted from supermarkets too; it was a sport. Sometimes they went to eat somewhere and left without paying, just ran off, thrilled with their thieving. They took advantage of crowds in shopping malls to snatch old ladies' purses, and they extorted younger students, in grades 3 and 4, into stealing from their parents and giving them the money so they'd leave them alone—it was totally evil.

So it was an accident that Mara was walking near them as they all came back from the sports field that afternoon. She usually tried to avoid them, but not because she was afraid. They'd never done anything to her—nobody had ever stolen anything from her—or tried to extort her. Mara knew the girls respected her. And she wanted it to stay that way.

So she'd had to do something when on the way back from the field, Rosa suddenly said, "You are my friend, aren't you?"

The four absolutely loved that. They slapped their thighs, shrieked and roared, "Rosa the whale is Mara's friend! No way! Insane!"

Because she hadn't wanted to stand for that, couldn't stand for that, she'd just looked briefly at Rosa and then the gang and said, "Whale? Really? Let's see your blubber bounce then." She stretched out her foot and kicked out.

She didn't like to remember the scene, although it had reinforced her position as the cool one, not to be messed with. They were on their way back to school after a tiring afternoon. It was hot and there was a storm brewing. They had all been training for sports day in a few weeks' time, apart from Rosa—she was allowed to spend an entire hot afternoon sitting on the bleachers, sucking ice cubes and giving them advice. They'd all found it sickening that they'd had to sweat like pigs while the fat cow lazed about. Rosa hadn't brought her gym clothes, as usual, despite the fact that she was the one who really needed the exercise! But the teachers just accepted it by now.

Mara had been aiming for her thigh rather than her stomach, which still would have hurt but wouldn't have been as mean as what actually happened.

Rosa gasped for air and crumpled up immediately, her baggy T-shirt lying over her like a tent.

Then they ran away. The four girls and Mara. They'd left Rosa lying there, and Mara hadn't stopped to look back for a good few feet. By that time, Rosa was strenuously starting to lever herself off the ground and sit up.

Mara had felt a bit guilty, but Rosa was in school the next day and had smiled at her shyly. Mara nodded briefly. That was all, as if nothing had happened.

15

THREE STOPS LATER, TIM got on the bus. He looked around right away, as if he was searching for someone. Mara shrank down, but he'd already spotted her. A smile flitted across his face. He swung his backpack over his head as he came down the aisle toward her.

"Is this seat free?" he asked cheerfully. "I have to sit down. I'm wiped."

She took her backpack off the seat and pushed it under the one in front of her. Tim sat down. He still smelled a little of licorice. And he hadn't given up on his silly sideburns yet.

She turned away quickly, looked out the window.

"Hey," said Tim softly, "hello."

"Yeah, hello." Mara tried not to smile.

The guy just wouldn't give up. "Nice to see you," he said.

She just shrugged. She wasn't about to grin or say something stupid like nice to see you too. She thought that girls who always messed around with boys or constantly tried to flirt with them needed their heads examined. She never wanted to be like that, her head full of sentimental slush.

She slid closer toward the window, which made Tim watch her even more closely, as if he wanted to memorize every last pore on her skin. It made her pulse race.

"Can I tell you something?" he asked. "My last class was canceled today, and so I let two buses go by because I was sure you'd be on this one."

Mara slowly turned her head toward him, a deep furrow on her brow.

And now, she thought, almost grinning at the idea, your meal will be cold when you get home.

He laughed. "You must be thinking, What an idiot!"

"No," said Mara, "I don't think that."

"What are you thinking then?"

"Me?"

Tim looked around. "Do you get the feeling I'm talking to a ghost?"

"Perhaps."

"You're a weird girl," said Tim. "Mute as a fish."

The bus rounded a corner.

"But I like that."

"What?" asked Mara.

"Everything. How you are. Quiet. Cool. Cocky." He smiled. "And exciting."

She was so surprised that she looked at him properly now. He had green eyes with blue flecks in them. Strange, like the sea and the sky coming together, she thought and wondered where the idea had come from. Later I'll study my eyes and see how many colors are in them. Perhaps there are even more dabs of color than in this guy's. She thought that the mole wasn't as noticable as the first time they'd met. Has he smeared something on it? Mara wondered. He thinks I'm exciting. Why exciting?

Then he asked her what she was doing next Wednesday afternoon.

"Why then?"

"That's the only afternoon I have free, really. There's always something going on. My manic family is constantly busy." He groaned slightly and then told her about his sister: she had ballet on Monday, flute lessons on Tuesday, a computer course on Wednesday, confirmation classes on Thursday, and swimming practice on Friday. His sister was named Sophie. And he had something nearly every day, but he'd managed to keep one afternoon free. So if she happened to have nothing better to do next week...

He didn't finish the sentence. Mara's head was spinning as she tried to hide her excitement.

Tim was the first boy she'd ever let ask her out. She had got so used to thinking boys were stupid, to brushing them off coolly. But now Tim was sitting next to her and practically suggesting a date and it felt totally natural. But something in her didn't want to give way on her principles. And that "something" was so hard to overcome.

"What did you have in mind?" she asked calmly.

"No idea." He laughed. "It was probably a dumb idea, wasn't it? We don't even know each other."

"True," she answered, thinking, Why am I talking such crap?! She looked through the window. There were still two or three stops until he got off, and she considered how she could keep the conversation going until then without it looking like being friendly. She couldn't think of anything. She suddenly remembered about Rosa Riccione's mother and what she might have said. It was a bad idea to think about that. Then she remembered that her mother had asked her to get painkillers from the drugstore for her. Had she still got the three dollars that that would probably cost?

And suddenly the bus was slowing down and Tim was saying, "I've got to get off here."

Mara was startled. So soon?

They looked at each other. She just didn't know what to say.

"Okay," she managed in the end. "Bye, then."

"Yes," he said slowly, "bye." He got up. He held tightly on to the pole and looked down at her. "You didn't answer me. Are you free next Wednesday?" he asked.

"I've . . . I'm busy," said Mara hastily. She gave a cool smile and shrugged. "Sorry."

He looked serious. Now his eyes looked even more gorgeous. "In that case," he said. "If you're busy . . . then it's too bad."

She nodded.

The bus pulled up to the curb and the driver watched Tim in the rearview mirror. Tim gestured that he wanted to go on another stop, so the driver grinned and pulled out again.

"Ha," laughed Tim. "Saved. Another stop."

He put his bag on the seat and pulled out his cell phone. "In case anything comes up," he said, "I'll give you my number."

"You can't," said Mara. "I haven't got a phone."

He dropped his arm and stared at her.

"You ... haven't ... got a phone?"

Mara shook her head. "It was stolen," she said. That was a lie, but it was better than the truth. She had had to give her phone back a few months before. When you can't pay the rent, there's no money for unnecessary phone calls. That's what her father said.

They'd fought like cat and dog about that, Mara and her father. She had screamed at him that, in that case, perhaps he could give up his beer and whisky down at the bar or her mother could give up her lousy cigarettes. She hadn't let her cell phone out of her sight after that; she'd slept with it under her pillow, taken it into the bathroom and the kitchen with her. But it had still somehow disappeared one morning and she'd had no idea when her father could have got hold of it. It had just gone.

Tim stared at her until the bus stopped again, as if he couldn't believe he was falling for a girl who didn't have a phone.

Mara had jammed her hands between her knees because she didn't want him to notice they were shaking.

"See you sometime, then," said Tim.

She nodded.

He took his backpack, smiled at the driver, and jumped off the bus. The bus drove on and Mara leaned her head against the glass. She didn't look back. God, she thought, he's so sweet. Why the hell am I so ... so knotted up?!

16

MARA'S MOTHER WAS SITTING in her bed, propped up on piles of cushions, and flicking through one of Mara's magazines with her left hand. She'd put on a pop CD and looked at her daughter with pleasure and a certain expectation.

As soon as she'd got in, Mara had gone straight to the kitchen to make herself something to eat. Now she was standing in her bedroom door because her mother needed to speak to her urgently. Whenever Beth got excited, her face broke out in red blotches, and it was like that now. Mara listened: they were going to rearrange the apartment. Her mother had decided and evidently forced her father to agree to it while she'd been at school.

"You don't need to sleep on the sofa anymore," she said. "That's no good anyway, if Dad wants to watch his stupid films at night. You can have our room."

"Your room? What use is that? I don't want your room." Mara was holding a package of noodles in her hand and trying to read the instructions. It was all she'd been able to find to eat in the kitchen cupboards. Even the instant soups had been used up.

"It's not a light room, but it's bigger than yours, and it faces away so you wouldn't hear the TV from the living room all night."

"Mom," shouted Mara indignantly, "I've got a room. I don't want your bedroom!"

Her mother laughed with a strain.

"I can't sleep in the same bed as your father anymore," she whispered. "I can't get any rest like that, every time he turns over or talks in his sleep I think—"

"What?" asked Mara.

"That he's going to do something, you know. And when he's been drinking and stinks like that... I can't bear it. Sweetie, please. I need a room with a lock."

Mara looked at her mother, looked at her desk, at the basket with woolen socks underneath it, at the heap of clean clothes next to the closet, at the pinboard. She shook her head.

"It's my room," she said. "It's the only place that belongs to me, the only reason I can stand it in this lousy apartment."

"Your father will sleep on the sofa," said her mother without taking any notice of her outburst. She coaxed her. "He won't bother you!"

"Mom! I don't want to go into your bedroom! It gives me the creeps! Don't you get it?"

Beth looked at her. Enormous eyes, ringed with black, in a pale face.

"I can't cope anymore, sweetie," she whispered. "Can't you see? I'm cracking up!"

"Then do something about it, for God's sake, anything!" Mara was fighting against tears of rage and frustration. She swallowed them down.

Her mother turned to the wall and pulled the covers over her head. Mara stood in the door, the package of noodles in her hand, waiting. For an answer, for anything. But her mother said nothing else.

Then Mara hurled the noodles against the wall. And waited some more. But her mother didn't even twitch. She didn't move under Mara's duvet.

17

MARA PROWLED AROUND the city.
No way! No way were they doing that! She had
nowhere in the apartment where she could hide away, disappear. Vanish altogether!

Nowhere that smelled the way she liked it, where it could
be as bright or cozily dim as she wanted it to be at any moment, with all her own things. No bed that belonged to her,
which she'd made warm and which smelled of her body.

Mara had a shower every day with a gorgeous shower gel;
it almost smelled like the white lilies when they opened at
the florist's. She sometimes passed the store and when the
lilies were in bloom, she could hang around for hours just
breathing in their scent.

But there weren't any lilies at the moment. It was the
wrong time of year for them. There wouldn't be any until
December, January, when they were flown in from the
tropics or some hothouse in southern Europe or somewhere. But there were shower gels to make up for it. And
she wanted one. Now!

Mara stopped outside the supermarket door. Shopping carts were parked near the entrance and there was a red elephant that bounced up and down when you stuck a coin in the slot. A little boy was sitting on the elephant, his cheeks puffed up with excitement. I bet he's got his own room, she thought. The boy's mother was standing nearby and watching tenderly as her child enjoyed himself. He's got everything he needs, thought Mara. But perhaps he prefers to sleep in his parents' bed. He's only little.

She stormed into the supermarket. The front shelves were full of dog food, cat food, cleaning products, toilet paper, paper towels. She turned to a clerk bending down to sort something out on one of those shelves. "Shower gel?" she asked.

The clerk got up slowly. She put her hand on her back; she was no longer particularly young.

"Can't you ask politely?" She looked at Mara reproachfully.

"Where is the shower gel?" Mara spat.

"We've got hundreds of varieties," answered the woman. "What sort do you want, maybe...?"

Suddenly Mara was so pissed off that she didn't let the woman finish. She banged into her so roughly that the woman almost fell over and then Mara stomped on.

"Hey! You!" the outraged clerk called after her. "Where are your manners? I'll call the manager..."

Mara didn't care. She brushed her hand past a tall pyramid of chocolate figures. The structure collapsed and the figures rolled all over the floor. A man turned around and stared at her but said nothing. Perhaps he's stealing something, she thought.

The shower gel was in the next aisle. She knew what she was looking for, what her favorite bottles looked like. But there was a gaping hole on the shelf just where it should have been.

Everything was there except her lily shower gel! The one thing she needed right now!

It filled her with such rage that she could hardly think. She felt as if the veins were bursting in her eyes and a red mist was covering her pupils. She could hardly see as she stretched out her hand and swept everything off the shelves: all the shower gels and bubble baths, all the deodorants and sprays, aftershaves and shampoos.

Whatever. Everything must go, all onto the floor, there should be total chaos, she wanted people to get mad and shout and screech and try to catch her, to tie her down, to lock her up, but they wouldn't do it. Mara felt a vast energy in herself, a fury like never before.

Look what comes of taking away my room, she thought, see what it gets you. It was ridiculous, somewhere deep inside she knew that, but she couldn't help it. Then she ran for the exit.

Suddenly someone shouted, "Stop! For God's sake! What's going on?" A man with a name badge on his chest stood in her way, his arms outstretched.

But Mara was lightning fast. She simply dived under his arms and was out of the store before anybody could react, before anyone could chase after her and corner her.

She was already across the road, around the corner, and away.

She was breathing hard and it took a long time before her heartbeat calmed down. Then a warm wave flowed through her body, sweeping away the anger, and she was calmer. At last. She could see normally again, think normally. All that was left of what had just happened inside her was a vague inkling. It was like after a storm, when it's still rumbling around but the sky is light and clear again.

She roamed around the city some more, went into the park, to the kids' playground, and sat on a bench with the young mothers and watched the children playing for a while. Perhaps I can learn something for next week, she thought, for the day-care center. But then it started to spit with rain, just a few drops, and the playground emptied.

Mara walked on. She looked at her watch every half-hour. Time dragged. She didn't have enough money for a movie. She was broke except for the money for her monthly bus pass.

As she passed a busy donair stall, somebody called her name.

She stopped. Crowded around one of the little stand-up bistro tables with a red waxed cloth tacked to it were the gang of four grade 9 girls. They had mountains of food piled up in front of them. They raised their pop cans to Mara from across the street and extravagantly wiped their mouths with the backs of their hands. It looked gross.

Helena waved to her. "Hey, Mara, what a coincidence."

Mara had no desire to join them. She eyed the girls scornfully and made to walk on.

"Hey, hang on!" called Laura. "Seeing as you're here, we want to discuss something with you!"

Mara hesitated. She looked down the road. Four older trees that hadn't survived the cold winter needed to be cut down — the sight of tall, bare trees at the end of spring was strangely depressing. It looked like the trees were going to be felled today. A truck with a crane was just arriving and a couple of men jumped out of the cab.

"What do you want?" Reluctantly she approached them. She looked at the table: the paper plates with donairs on them; the salad, fresh and finely chopped; the garlic sauce and pickles. The crispy bread smelled of sesame seeds. She felt her stomach contract and could hardly tear her eyes away from the food.

Sara spotted it. "Hungry?" she asked invitingly. "It's great. We always come here."

Sara was the smartest in the gang. Before she'd joined them, she'd done well at her previous school. But then her parents split up because they'd met other people — in a swingers club, of all places — and both wanted to start new lives, just like that. During the divorce, it had become clear that neither of Sara's parents nor their new partners wanted her to live with them. But the family judge reminded her mother of her duty. To Sara he said, "It wasn't that easy to persuade your mother to take you into her new life. But she now understands that she must look after you. The alternative would be a home. Do you want to go into a home?" That was the day Sara's childhood ended. She started to skip school, stopped doing her homework, didn't study for tests, let herself go, drifted around the city. At the age of thirteen, she had a boyfriend ten years older who made her have sex with his friends and he kept the money. That lasted until her mother finally told the children's services office, who banned the boyfriend from ever contacting her again.

Sara was the only one of the four that Mara felt any kind of similarity with. She had heard the rumors when Sara first arrived at school and was suddenly thrown in among the students, eyed suspiciously. It was Sara who first "made something" of the gang. Everyone knew that. Sara, who had no mercy on the little kids, who ruthlessly extorted anyone who showed the least weakness and didn't fight back.

Mara joined the girls at the table. Helena asked her what she'd like to eat. "We'll get you something," she boasted.

Normally Mara wouldn't have accepted anything. But today she nodded. Her stomach was one big hole. She felt sick. If she had something in her belly she'd feel better.

She and Helena chose a donair with all the trimmings and came back to the table with a can of Coke.

On the table, among all the paper plates and used napkins, lay four brand-new cell phones, all with digital cameras, tiny silver things that you could open and snap shut, the latest models.

"Where'd you get them from?" asked Mara. She felt something like envy. She'd have loved one of those phones. The four of them looked at one another. "Yeeaah … where did we get them?" drawled Laura, and the others snorted with laughter.

Mara kept cool. She didn't join in their stupid laughter.

Nadine wiped her eyes.

"Our parents aren't exactly millionaires, if that's what you mean. We got them for ourselves."

"We can always find a way to get what we need," said Sara. And then she laughed again.

Mara ate her donair in silence, drank her Coke, and watched as the crane went up in the distance with one of the men from the truck standing in a bucket and starting to lop off the top branches of the dead tree. A heavy branch was fixed with a rope, and she could hear the whine of a saw. The next minute the dead limb crashed to the ground, where it split.

"We're just wondering," said Sara, "whether we should expand our gang. More members means more income! More girls like us means more success!" she explained. "Do you get me?"

"No."

"Well." Sara rolled her eyes. "I dream of really laying into the boys' gangs, not just the guys at Brentwood, they're pretty lame," she grinned. "I mean the city gangs."

"We think it's totally shit"—Nadine took over now— "that people only ever have respect for the boys, that only guys get to say what's what."

"It's time for us women to get into the big time," chimed in Laura. "So Sara thinks we should expand."

"But we only want the best," added Nadine. "And we know that you're good. We could do loads together, today this neighborhood, tomorrow the world!" She laughed at her joke. The others joined in.

"We saw that the other day," grinned Helena. "You know, with the fat cow, Rosa Riccione! What do you think? Will you join us?"

Mara said nothing, kept eating her donair. She looked at the old trees, which were getting smaller and smaller. She didn't know what she should say, or rather how to say it; she thought for a while.

Finally she said, "I think it's pathetic to rip off little kids who can't defend themselves."

The others watched her. Waited.

"Honestly," said Mara. "There's no pride in beating up kids. Scaring them. I think it's stupid."

"You're saying you think what we're doing is shit?" Helena dragged the sentence out, a threatening edge in her tone.

Mara stayed calm. "Yeah, pretty much. I don't care what your plans are. But I think it's wrong to snatch an old lady's purse or to extort money from the old guy in the corner store. Totally wrong."

The four of them didn't speak. Mara finished her meal. The girls were still silent.

Then finally Helena said, "What about you? You're always screwing things up. What makes you so smug?"

"I'm not smug."

"No? Not at all? You're proud of smacking people's faces in, aren't you?"

Mara realized there was no point talking to them. The girls just didn't get it. They had no idea. They just thought about crap like digital cameras and what they could get with their dirty money.

If Mara was honest, she didn't need all that. A phone you could take pictures with. Photos of what? Her father? Or her mother lying in bed, bawling? The empty beer cans under the kitchen table?

The others were still staring at her, waiting for something.

But Mara didn't want to talk to them anymore.

"That it?" she asked.

Sara nodded.

Mara smiled and waved. "Bye, then!" she said, strolling away.

18

MARA SPENT HALF THE night meandering around the city on the buses. She didn't want to go home. She didn't want to go back to her parents' bedroom. She dreaded the double bed, the carpet, the curtains, her father's old felt slippers under the bed with the collected foot odors of decades. She couldn't even think about it.

At some point they passed the bus stop near where Tim lived. She got off. She still had no idea where Cudworth Way was. So she wandered around the unfamiliar streets, looked into strange gardens, illuminated windows, heard the barking of dogs and the opening and closing of garage doors. Occasional music. It was a peaceful area. No bars, no questionable clubs, no weeds, no graffiti on the walls. A picture-book area. She took the last bus home.

THE MAIL WAS STILL in the box. Among all the junk, there was a white envelope with the school stamp on it. It was addressed to Mara Dolan, 178 Wilson Street. To her personally! The school office normally wrote to her parents. Ominous letters, bad grades, having to repeat a year, parents' evenings, consultations...

She sat down on the stairs and read the letter. It was long and hand-written. It was from Mrs. Sidler.

Dear Mara,

I am sorry to say that I had a very unsatisfactory conversation today in relation to you. I immediately tried to call you at home, but your telephone isn't working. (Yes, thought Mara. That'll be because the bill hasn't been paid.) *So I have to try to reach you like this. Before your work experience placement, which begins on Monday.*

Mara, I'm disappointed, horrified, and at my wits' end. I have no idea what to do with you anymore. Why are you always hurting other people? Do you think it'll help you in any way, that it'll make your situation any better?

If you don't learn to manage your anger and frustration properly, you'll have to leave the school. And no other school will take you!

That can happen more quickly than you think. And what will you do without any qualifications? Hang around? That would be the beginning of a very slippery slope...

This time, as I'm sure you're aware, it's a matter of an inexcusably brutal attack on one of your classmates. If only I'd known about the incident! In any case, Rosa Riccione's mother threatened to press charges against you!

Do you realize the gravity of the situation now?!

I was furious when Mrs. Riccione told me about you and

Rosa. Rosa wants to be your friend! She keeps trying. She's given you presents (Yes, thought Mara, one tampon), *helped you out, seeks out your company. She has forgiven you when you've lost it with her, as she calls it. Again and again! And while the others laughed at Rosa, it was you who hit her! You laughed at her tears. You were indifferent to her pain. Mara! Have you no pity? No feelings for others?*

I am your homeroom teacher and I tell you that I will not have such things going on in my class!

You are old enough, Mara, to be legally responsible for your actions. And that means that a court could punish you for these incidents. I don't believe that you would find any judge who'd be as lenient with you as I've been as your teacher. I still want to have faith in you, despite everything…

Mara, I think you recognized how much I've put myself out to get this work placement at the day-care center for you. I am now doubly worried—is it responsible of me to entrust you with small children? However, I want to give you one last chance. I will believe one last time in the good potential that is in you, but that must not be buried any deeper.

Make the best of this placement! Show the goodness in you! Everything depends on this now. Absolutely everything! I will use these two weeks to try to placate Rosa's mother.

This is the last thing I will do for you.

Your teacher, Mrs. Suzanne Sidler

Mara scrunched the two sheets of paper together and hurled them against the wall.

19

IN THE APARTMENT, THE only light was the bluish shimmer of the television. The sound was turned off. Her father was sleeping in his clothes on the sofa, one hand hanging down, empty beer cans around him on the floor.

She got undressed in the bathroom, wrapped herself in her dressing gown, and went into her parents' bedroom.

She crawled into the bed; it was cold and smelled of cigarette smoke. The bedclothes had obviously not been changed, and her father's musty pajamas lay rolled up under the thin pillow next to her. Revolted, she hurled the pajamas to the floor, then rewrapped herself up to her nose in her dressing gown and pulled the covers over her.

She lay on her back, her eyes clenched shut, because everything in the bedroom depressed her. She kept her breathing very shallow so that her chest hardly rose or fell.

She imagined what it would be like to be dead, what it would be like if her parents came into the room the next morning with no idea, stood at the edge of the bed and stared at their daughter's corpse. She wondered how her mother would react. And her father.

Then she thought about Tim. It was nice to imagine him standing by her bed, like the prince who has awoken Sleeping Beauty, behind the hundred-year-old hedge of roses, out of her hundred-year sleep, with just one kiss. She imagined that one kiss would transform her into somebody else, beautiful and wild but good nonetheless.

When she woke up the next morning, the sheet was damp with blood. She had forgotten to change her tampon the night before. What a great start to the day. Then she reconsidered the letter from Mrs. Sidler. That confirmed it. She wasn't going to school today. Like her parents would even notice.

By 10:00 a.m., when her mother, groggy with sleep, came out of Mara's room, Mara had already stuffed the sheet and the dressing gown into the washing machine, cleaned the bloodstain on the mattress with soap and a nailbrush, and then heaved the mattress to the open window. Her father had left the apartment early; Mara had heard the door slam. Perhaps one of his old friends had offered him an odd job somewhere. Or he'd gone straight to the bar.

Her mother made coffee.

"There's nothing to eat but two packages of noodles and ketchup," said Mara.

The only answer was a sigh. "I know."

"How are we going to go on like this?"

"Your father's got work today. Clearing out a garage. And he's going to social services on Monday," she answered. "To apply for welfare. I hope we'll get money again soon. For the outstanding rent, and maybe the phone..." She broke off.

"And you?" asked Mara.

"What about me?"

"Well, what are you going to do? Welfare won't be enough."

Her mother sat at the kitchen table. "What do you want me to do?"

"I don't know!" she almost shouted. "There must be some kind of job. That would be good for you too..." and she added "...if you won't go to the doctor!" She thumped the table with her fist and her mother clutched at her injured shoulder in shock. "I'm so shattered, honey," she gasped in the end, "totally shattered. Work... I don't think I can cope anymore."

"Mom!" Mara lowered her voice. "How old are you?"

"I know how old I am, only forty-four." She groaned. "But sometimes I feel older, sometimes younger, I feel about a hundred. I can hardly get out of bed. Yesterday afternoon the doorbell rang. But I didn't answer. I went to the window and looked through the curtains. I saw a woman leaving the building. She was wearing a red velvet jacket. I thought for a moment it was that... what's-her-name... that teacher of yours."

At that moment, Mara remembered the letter. She thanked her lucky stars her mother hadn't opened the door. When she imagined Mrs. Sidler here in the apartment...

"And you? Where were you last night? You came home late. Were you out with your friends?" She stretched out her left arm with a smile and stroked Mara's fingers.

If only her mother knew! Out with friends! Which friends would that be? And where on earth could they have gone? Did she have any money for the movies? For a club? She wanted to say something, but when she saw the pale hand touching her so helplessly, so sadly, she left it.

When was the last time her mother had laughed out loud? When had she said anything cheerful? Danced to music? Or hummed along with a song? When had she last had any fun?

Her life hadn't always been like this. At some point it had started going off track, after which it had gradually worsened, like an indefinable illness. Every time something happened—the accident, her father's first bout of unemployment, or when Simone left—she went downhill faster. And now it was like this: a father who drank, a mother who hid herself away. A sister who sent postcards. How have I endured it? thought Mara. All these years, how, for God's sake? She pitied her mother and was afraid of her father. No, "afraid" was the wrong word; she tried not to annoy him or to contradict him. It didn't do any good. Her father wouldn't take backtalk, he wouldn't take questions, reproof. He wanted to be master in his own home and she was to obey him. Especially when he'd been drinking.

He drank to forget that he didn't really have a grip on his life. Mara could sense that without needing to be told. He hadn't finished his education and remained a toolmaker all his life.

"He feels like a failure," her mother had said once, "be-cause he really wanted to make something of his life. My

God, when I think of how he promised me the moon when we first met. And? Look what he's become."

Her father was tall, almost six feet six, and when he was younger he'd been a boxer. The trainers thought he had talent. But at some point he'd flattened a man outside the boxing ring, someone who'd wanted to steal his girlfriend. After that he was barred from the club and not allowed in the ring. The trainers dropped him like a hot potato and his fellow fighters didn't want anything to do with him. Her father had once said that his boxing time had been the best time of his life.

If she really tried, Mara could imagine Gary Dolan as a teenager, when the girls flocked around him, when he was a star boxer. He would have felt like a hero, in his club back home, the strongest in his weight category. Perhaps believing that they'd roll out the red carpet for him, the man in the ring...

Sometimes Mara thought about her grandparents, her father's parents. Gertrude and John Dolan, from a small village where they'd had a butchery, along with a big house, right on the banks of a little lake. They had a large fruit orchard and a meadow with sheep grazing themselves plump and fat in summer. There were reeds and a dock with a rowboat tied up to it. Mara knew that from the photos in the brown album. You could see it all in the photos: the gables of the half-timbered house, the beautiful lattice windows, the archway through which you entered the premises, the large windows of the butchery, over which it read, DOLAN BUTCHERY.

For the photo, her grandparents had positioned them-selves in the entrance; the light was bright behind them.

Then the living room: photographed without flash on a sunny day, light slanting through the windows, heavy oak furniture. Not Mara's style, but it looked cozy. And tidy. It looked as if the people who lived there were happy. Then the summerhouse entwined with vine leaves. Everything lovingly photographed, as if to capture it for eternity. A garden table with a basket of apples, next to it in the grass a stone figurine. A little girl holding out her skirt as if to catch a falling star; a few red autumn leaves lay in the outstretched skirt.

There were autumn leaves on the steps down to the dock too; a little white dog was jumping down them and barking at the camera.

The parents had sent the album to their son. Without a note. They had sent it to him so he would know what he'd lost when he left them behind.

It was a farewell gift. Not long afterward, Mara's grandparents had died. Her father had not traveled to the funeral—he said travel was too expensive and, anyway, there was no reason to. He hadn't visited his parents while they were still alive, so there was no reason for him to act as if everything was normal between them now.

So he only sent a wreath. According to Beth, he was furi-ous that his parents had disinherited him.

They had wanted him to take over their small butch-ery one day, but he'd never intended to—he'd wanted to do something else, something bigger. But it never came to anything. Perhaps, she thought, he had been too ashamed to face his parents because he'd never really amounted to anything. That that was why he'd broken away from them altogether.

And it had never occurred to him that it might be nice for his daughters, for Simone and Mara, to have grandparents to visit, grandparents who care, who are just kind.

"Didn't my grandparents ever see me or Simone, even as babies?" Mara had asked.

"No."

"Did you send them a photo of me?"

"No, we didn't."

"Why not?"

"He didn't want to."

"What about Simone?"

"No, we didn't then either."

It had been a strange conversation. Her mother had shaken her head in answer to all the questions and resignedly shrugged her shoulders, which had driven Mara totally mad.

"Did they even know we existed?" she yelled in the end. Her mother had looked at her and silently shaken her head.

Then they hadn't spoken another word. All you could hear was the turning of the pages, the rustling of the paper between the card pages displaying the photos. That was the first moment Mara felt the fireball in her head and the urge to destroy something. Because—as she knew today—she was afraid of being destroyed herself.

She had been ten. The year she started fighting in the playground and dunking other children in the swimming pool until they almost drowned. The time she cut off half the long, fat braid of a girl in her art class when nobody was looking, the severed end lying on the floor like a yellow snake. The year she snatched the bags from a group of younger kids, threw them up into the air, and then stamped on them with all her might. Until everything was broken. Just because.

20

I**T WASN'T EASY TO** find the day-care center. It was housed in a complex—a giant maze of a clinker building with two central courtyards—that had once been a vinegar factory and was now used by loads of small companies.

Mara just followed a young woman who was pulling two crying girls of about three years of age behind her. They were obviously twins and dressed identically.

They crossed the first courtyard, in which old bits of machinery stood as if it was an open-air museum, then went down a broad corridor, tiled in green and white, into the second courtyard. A dump truck was just unloading a batch of fresh sand for the playground; two workmen were spreading the sand over the wide surface.

As she passed, Mara glimpsed a slide, a swing, monkey bars. The two three-year-olds kept crying the whole time, but the mother, holding their hands, didn't take any notice. She just pulled the girls behind her in silence. Perhaps this was repeated every morning and she didn't feel like explaining to them every time that the day-care center was good for them. And that anyway, there was no choice. Probably the young woman had to go straight from here to work.

There was a small crowd in the entrance. Mara watched the mother as she took the two little girls' jackets off while talking to another woman, who had an even younger girl in her arms. In the background, two boys were hitting each other with their lunchboxes until another child separated them.

There was a cloakroom with lockers adorned with animal pictures. There were indoor shoes in the lockers. The outdoor shoes, on the other hand, lay in chaotic heaps on the floor.

It smelled of fresh coffee and warm rolls. Mara suddenly felt her empty stomach.

The young woman kissed the two girls, who were gradually calming down, stroked their hair, and left. A boy of about five years of age stormed into the building, yelling, "Hey! Here comes King Kong!" and let out a wild cry. The telephone in the main room was ringing. A little boy, in the middle of the room, was trying to pull down his pants. The kindergarten teacher walked past him; she was balancing the breakfast dishes as she walked through the room. The boy looked at her and said, "Pooh-pooh!"

The teacher whirled round. "No, Danny! Quick, to the toilet!" She put the cups down, raced over to him, picked up the fidgeting boy by the shoulders, and carried him out of the room, his pants still halfway down.

Suddenly a cold hand was thrust into her hand. "Will you help me with my shoes?"

Next to her stood a girl of about four with corkscrew curls and snot trickling from her nose.

"Of course," said Mara, bending down quickly.

The girl watched from above as Mara untangled the knots in her shoelaces. She screwed up her nose.

"Haven't you got a Kleenex?" asked Mara.

The girl shook her head. "Mommy always forgets."

"I think I've got one."

Mara couldn't stand kids with runny noses. She dug in her jeans for a Kleenex and held it under the girl's nose. The girl looked at her with big eyes.

"Blow!" ordered Mara.

The girl pushed her hand away firmly. "Can't."

"Course you can. Come here." Mara noticed that the girl was afraid of her size and her loud voice. She crouched down, softened her voice. "We hold one nostril shut, see? Then you take a deep breath and push it out through the other nostril. And all the boogers come out with it. I'll show you them afterward."

"In your Kleenex?" asked the girl.

"That's right." Mara nodded cheerfully.

"And then do you eat them?" asked the girl. The kid was so cute that Mara just gave her a hug. "You don't eat stuff like that, that's yucky," she whispered in her ear.

The girl giggled. "It tickles when you talk."

"What's your name?"

"Katie."

"Hello, Katie."

"What's yours?"

"Mara."

"Who's your child?"

"I haven't got a child," said Mara with a smile. "I'm going to work here for two weeks."

"You're going to look after us today?" Katie's eyes began to shine.

Mara put her head on one side. "Would you like that?"

The girl looked at her seriously. "Can you play with children?"

Mara thought back to when she and Simone had played for hours and had totally forgotten everything else around them. "Me? Of course I can! I'm the Champion Children's Games Inventor! I'm famous for it!—Maralise, the Games Fairy." Maralise, that's what Simone used to call her. "Can't you tell?"

Katie looked at her quietly. Mara pulled a few faces and then Katie laughed.

"Well? What do you think?" asked Mara. "Can I stay?"

Katie took her hand and pulled her proudly behind her through the room, to the kindergarten teacher, who was just sitting the boy—with his pants on now—on a chair and pushing it under the table.

There was a plate at every place, with a jam roll and a jug of milk.

"Mrs. Clement! You don't have to look after us today!" Katie tugged at the teacher's sweater until at last she turned around. And they both looked at her, first Katie and then Mara. She raised her eyebrows and smiled. Mara smiled back.

"What did you say, Katie?" The woman bent down to the girl.

"You can go home. Maralise will look after us. And play super games with us!" Katie took Mara's hand again.

"Maralise sounds sweet!" Mrs. Clement held out her hand. "You must be Mrs. Sidler's student and your real name is Mara Dolan."

Mara blushed a little and nodded.

The teacher spread out her arms in welcome. "Well then, this is your workplace for the next two weeks." She raised her voice. "It's quite noisy, isn't it?"

"It's louder on the school grounds," replied Mara.

"Really? I wouldn't have thought that was possible," laughed the teacher. She smiled again.

Mara guessed that Mrs. Clement was in her early fifties. She was tall and thin and had a long, narrow face, which looked strict as soon as the smile disappeared. She seemed like someone who was very stressed but didn't want to show it. You could tell that she took her profession very seriously.

She brought out a gong from a cupboard and struck it twice. Immediately, the volume level dropped considerably.

"Come on, children, hold hands, and then we'll all say good morning!"

The children slowly stretched out their hands to the left and the right without really looking. Katie was sitting between a boy with freckles and a girl with glasses. She pushed the girl away when she tried to hold her hand and stood up and gave the freckled boy a smacking kiss. That made the girl next to her start to cry and the boy hit Katie in the stomach. Mrs. Clement had spotted it.

"Carlos! I never want to see that again! Did you just hit Katie?"

Carlos crossed his arms over his chest with a defiant glare.

"And Katie!" cried Mrs. Clement. "Sit down again! That's what happens when you don't do as I tell you!"

Katie sat down, pushed her plate away, put her head on the table, and buried her face.

Mara wanted to go to her, but Mrs. Clement held her back.

"Just ignore it," she murmured. "If you go to her now, she'll lead you by the nose forever. They're only putting it on for your benefit. They love having new people around. They'll soon calm down. I'll tell them who you are in a minute, then it'll be over."

She clapped her hands, waited until they were all looking at her, and introduced Mara to the group.

"But her name's Maralise!" Katie interrupted twice. In the end, Mara said, "Okay, my name's Maralise."

Katie smiled proudly at that and leaned back in her chair. She looked round triumphantly.

Mara couldn't keep her eyes off Katie. She just liked the girl with her turned-up nose, her shining brown eyes, and her corkscrew curls. She was sweet. Was I ever such a happy, bright child? she wondered suddenly. It seemed fairly unlikely. As long as she could remember, she had felt the bad mood in her family, like a shadow. She couldn't have been a happy, even-tempered child—otherwise her father wouldn't have shut her in the cupboard when she was little. The clothes closet in the bedroom, the left side where her mother's clothes hung, had been the penalty box. Her older sister had also had to go there when she threw a tantrum, and Mara was shut in there if she shouted or caused trouble. But once, she'd managed to smuggle a screwdriver into the closet. She'd bored loads of little holes in the door, very carefully and quietly, so she got more air.

At some point the closet ended up being torn out and taken to the street for garbage collection. Mara remembered how her father had carried the thing in pieces down all five flights of stairs because the elevator had been out of order. He dumped it in the front garden where someone had helped themselves to the pieces before it could be taken away.

Mara had often imagined that closet with the holes bored in the door being rebuilt somewhere else and another child crouched inside it. Humming songs to herself to drive away the fear...

Mrs. Clement took Mara around the day-care, explaining the daily schedule and the jobs that needed doing. She showed her the washrooms with the tiny children's toilets, the low-level sinks, and all the toothbrush mugs adorned with animal pictures too; the nap room; the playroom that was padded throughout with foam; the kitchen and the storerooms.

The employees were forbidden to smoke, and between eight in the morning and four in the afternoon, when the last child was collected, there was no real break for the teachers.

"It's a long day," said Mrs. Clement, looking at Mara, "but we love our work. I presume you want to be a kindergarten teacher one day or you wouldn't have chosen to do your placement here. We're always glad when the school sends us really dedicated students who love working with small children, who want to take on the heavy responsibility we have here. We really don't want to be a last resort for people who can't think of anything else."

Mara hoped that Mrs. Clement couldn't see her blushing. But the kindergarten teacher was far too busy keeping an eye on all the exuberant boys and girls, answering five questions at once, wiping mouths and refilling juice cups to notice her. She called over to her: "Janine's in the kitchen. Will you go and introduce yourself? Janine's only just finished training, but she's good, she knows a lot. I'll come and have a quick coffee with you in a while, but then the doctor's coming. It looks as if there's a flu virus going around."

JANINE WAS NINETEEN, chubby-faced, and dressed in garish colors. She was wearing oversized plastic earrings. She had a little green nose-stud too. Her hair was inky black and she wore bright green shoes. She gave Mara a hug as affectionate as if she'd dreamt of meeting her all her life. Janine had a slight speech impediment, she lisped, but you soon got used to that. She said that Mrs. Clement was a great boss, just a bit stressed sometimes. But that was only natural because there was always something going on and, after all, Mrs. Clement was responsible for thirty-six children.

"We need loads more staff," said Janine, "to give the children more stimulation. You know, someone to play music for them or to demonstrate different instruments, perhaps even proper art classes or something. I sometimes think we ought to be doing lots more. We need more money. But the boss couldn't swing it. The center is partly funded by donations, and nowadays it's not so easy to get people to hand over a hundred dollars for kids' work. Mrs. Clement is scared stiff at the end of every month that there won't be enough money for the rent."

Oh God, thought Mara, that sounds familiar, even if it's not quite the same as at home.

Two women were working in the kitchen. They were preparing lunch, washing up the breakfast dishes, cleaning. Their names were Olive and Natasha.

Mara was hugged by them too and found out what was for lunch. Meatballs in a tasty tomato sauce and pasta. She was almost sick with hunger and could only just resist asking for one of the leftover breakfast rolls.

Olive and Natasha were nice. They told her that after the meal, when the children were having a nap, it was obviously a bit quieter here. Then you could sneak out for a couple of minutes. "You'll see," confided Olive, "it's nice here." She stroked Mara's cheek.

By lunchtime all the children were calling her Maralise, giving her endearing cuddles and pulling her around. Mara went from place to place with Janine, checking that all the children were eating properly and they weren't bothering their neighbors. She gave out desserts, supervised the kids as they brushed their teeth, helped them onto the toilets, wiped their bottoms. She soon felt really professional, and the hours passed a lot more quickly than at school.

The children beamed at her, always calling her by her new name "Maralise!" and clapped when she waddled like a duck or crowed like a rooster.

They wanted to sit on her lap, play with her hair, give her a kiss, and to know whether she'd come out of her mommy's tummy too.

Mrs. Clement grinned when she saw Mara getting on with the children, and Janine shared a bar of chocolate with her.

Mara listened to everything, noted what she needed to know about the course of the day, nodded and laughed. And she thought, Why is everyone here being so nice to me? I don't get it. But it was a great feeling.

21

IN THE APARTMENT, THE pictures on the walls were askew. The glass frames on two of them had cracked. The hall cupboard, which had been tippy since her father had kicked it, had been knocked over again and the contents of the drawers lay strewn around the place. Gloves, headbands, old key rings, a broken shoehorn. The board with the coat hooks was only hanging by one nail, Mara's denim jacket was lying on the floor.

"What's been going on here?" she cried. She felt panic rise up in her again. Her heart was pounding.

Nobody answered. The apartment was silent.

"Mom?" called Mara.

No answer.

"Dad?"

"I'm here. What are you shouting like that for?"

Her father was sitting on the sofa in his vest and pants, his feet on the coffee table. He was cutting his toenails and drinking beer. There was a porn video playing on the TV. With no sound. Mara stared at the screen and swallowed.

"Where've you been?" asked her father without looking up.

"At the day-care center."

He threw the nail scissors onto the table. "What the hell does that mean?" he roared.

"I was at the day-care center."

"What were you doing there?"

"Working."

He stared at her. His face was bright red.

"I told you, I don't want to hear shit like that!" he roared. "I'm your father, for God's sake, and you've got to respect me!"

"I do," replied Mara. And so as not to let the situation get out of control, she explained reluctantly that she was doing a work placement at the day-care center. From eight till four.

Her father opened another can. The beer sprayed out and foamed over the tattoo on his arm. He swore.

"Get a cloth!" he ordered.

She went into the kitchen, grabbed a cloth, and threw it into her father's lap.

"Where's Mom?" she asked.

"Out."

"Out?" repeated Mara suspiciously. "Again? She never goes out."

"Well, she's gone out now." Her father threw the cloth back at her; it landed at her feet.

Mara made no move to pick it up.

"Have you done anything to her?"

He snorted furiously. "What do I ever do to her? She shouldn't put on airs like that. She ought to clean this place up for once. It's a pigsty in here. See for yourself."

"Yes, your disgusting toenail clippings are all over the place. Can't you do that in the bathroom?" She didn't know why she was shouting. Her own voice rang in her ears like an echo, bouncing around inside her skull, and she could feel darting pains in her temples.

No, she thought, no, no, no!

She crossed into her room and slammed the door behind her.

Her mother's dirty clothes were still lying around. Her dressing gown was on the desk chair. Her brown shoes were next to the bed. Mara's magazines at its foot. The sheets and duvet were tangled up.

Furiously she hurled everything on the floor, pulled away the sheets and duvet, threw open the window. All at once she could hear birds chirping. Quite close, as if the sparrows were on her windowsill. Mara slammed the window shut again. The tweeting didn't fit events here.

Her mother wasn't in the bathroom or her bedroom.

Mara went back to her father. He had stopped the video and was staring vacantly at some baseball game or other on the sports channel. She stood in front of the television, forcing him to look at her.

"I want to know where she is, right now."

"Who?"

"Mom! For God's sake!"

"No idea."

"What happened here?" screamed Mara.

She thought, I don't want to know, I don't. But she asked anyway. Her head was a painful spinning-top. And the constant buzzing and roaring in her ears. She thought of Simone for a second. Where on earth was she, what was she doing now? It must be better than this. She almost couldn't breathe for the rage against her sister. She left me alone, she thought. It's me that ends up paying for all this. All this shit! Her father was unemployed and taking his frustration out on them, on the family—or what was left of it.

"You were fighting again, weren't you?"

"Maybe," he muttered. "I don't really remember. What else can you do with your mother? A crazy woman who won't leave the house."

"But she's gone now!"

"Yes, she's gone now."

Mara waited. Her heart thumped. "And where is she?"

Her father raised his head. His eyelids looked heavy and she could see that he'd had a lot to drink.

"Where is she? Gone to hell, for all I care. I sent her to hell. Have you got anything to eat?"

"Why would I have anything to eat? I've only just got home!"

Her father pulled over the pants that were lying next to him on the floor and fished around for his wallet. He took a crumpled ten-dollar bill and put it on the table. He smiled suddenly and, before Mara could stop him, he grabbed her hand. He had a strong grip. A boxer's grip. "We'll be all right, the two of us," he said. "I've still got a bit of money. We'll be all right."

She pulled her hand away. She saw that she was getting goose bumps, starting on that hand and then down her back.

"Buy something for us both. Something nice!" he said.

Mara grabbed the money before he had second thoughts. She was already at the door.

"Chicken wings," called her father, "with plenty of fries! A man could starve to death in this house!"

<hr/>

THE DOOR TO THE neighboring apartment opened as Mara came out into the stairwell. Mrs. Vrabec, her hair in curlers, the baby on her arm, blocked Mara's way. "If that happens again," she complained, "I will get police."

Mara wanted to get past, but Mrs. Vrabec held on to her left arm. The baby was sucking on a bit of bread.

"I don't know what happened," said Mara, her eyes on the floor. "I wasn't there."

"Your father, he is crazy," said Mrs. Vrabec. "He belongs in an asylum. Or in prison. If I had husband like that . . ."

The goose bumps. The ringing in her ears. "I've got to go," Mara mumbled and pulled away from her.

"Police should come!" Mrs. Vrabec called after her.

Mara ran down the stairs.

Okay, she thought, call the police, you stupid cow. If that's your idea of fun. Tell them my mother's gone. That nobody knows where. What she's doing. What's going on. That none of the Dolans can see through the chaos. That everything's a giant crock of shit . . .

She pulled the key ring out of her jacket pocket. She threw it around while silently screaming out her rage.

She came to the row of parked cars.

Okay, fine, the police, she thought, of course, why the hell not?

She took the Yale key for the main door, the one with a particularly sharp edge. The high-pitched scratching noise as the sharp metal gouged through the paint, scoring a long mark across a blue-gray Ford, did her good. She noticed the burning heat, the red anger, gradually subsiding in her head. She scratched the key along a black Kia and then a red Honda. And after each car she damaged, quite skilfully, quite inconspicuously, while pedestrians hurried past from time to time, she felt better.

22

EVERY MORNING AFTER BREAKFAST—when the weather was good—the kindergarten children walked in single file to the park, as they were doing today. Janine wore a red garden gnome-like hat, waving at the front, and Mara made sure that nobody dawdled at the back or got lost. Three sets of traffic lights, a little cul-de-sac, then the turnstile at the entrance to the park, through which each child had to be channeled one by one, and then they could see the big playground beneath the inviting chestnut trees. Much nicer than the courtyard at the day-care center.

Janine marched on ahead with a child holding each hand, and Mara brought up the rear, as ever accompanied by Katie.

The little girl was babbling on as usual, but Mara wasn't really listening to her today. She just said "uh-huh" or "mhmmh" and smiled occasionally, stroking her hair, because her thoughts were away with her mother. Judging by the appearance of the apartment when she'd got home yesterday, there must have been real trouble between her parents, her father must have reacted particularly violently. So her mother had had no choice but simply to up and leave. But it cut Mara to the quick that her mother hadn't left her anything, not even written the shortest note, nothing.

Was she going to run away like Simone?

Just leave?

Hide somewhere?

Whatever happened to her and her father?

Was that possible?

Why had her mother done such a thing?

This woman, of all people, who never left the house?

She decided to ask Mrs. Vrabec when she got home. She must have heard something.

It was extra nice in the park today. The birds were singing and it smelled of fresh, damp earth. Mara had always dreamt of having a garden as a child. A garden like her grandparents'. In the autumn she wished for an old garden table, heaped with red autumn leaves, just like in her grandparents' photos.

When she walked under tall, old trees (just like now) and the photos from the album popped into her mind, she always felt as if someone had excluded her from paradise. Not driven her out, because they hadn't even let her in in the first place. How lovely it must be to be allowed to live in a paradise like that. And how stupid and unfair it was that her father had thrown the chance away.

But she didn't want to think about it anymore. Not that again. God knows how many other things there were to worry about at the moment—things to do . . .

23

THE KIDS LOVED THE playground in this park, and all that went with it. They could take their shoes and socks off—so long as the sand wasn't too cold. They could roll on the grass, tumble, climb, gather leaves fallen from the bushes, and investigate rabbit holes.

Mara and Janine sometimes had to dry their tears, blow their noses, and apply bandages, or to settle fights and stop the little ones from chasing the ducks. But they could also hold their faces up to the sun, chew gum, and chat. Janine loved to talk. By the end of the first afternoon in the park, Mara knew practically everything about her.

Janine thought life was good. And had expectations for the future. She was totally happy with the children, and it exactly suited her skills and desires. But Mara could tell that there was something else she wanted, and wanted badly. Janine's favorite TV programs were talent shows, and Mara soon realized that Janine still hoped to be discovered one day. The only thing Mara couldn't see in her was any of the necessary talent. Lisping wasn't really a talent that you could turn into a career . . . Although Janine was older than her, she seemed more childish. Somehow enviable.

Mara had to smile, thinking back to it now. But she didn't get any further with her thoughts about Janine, the budding kindergarten teacher.

Katie piped up.

The little girl's affection for Mara was apparent. Even when she was playing with the other children, she would stop and look questioningly around for her. If she couldn't see her right away, she pulled a face and called for her, dropped the bucket and shovel, and wouldn't move until Mara picked her up or messed around with her for a bit.

"I don't want to play today," said Katie, reaching for Mara's hand.

"Oh, what do you want to do then?"

"Stay with you." She cast a melting look at her.

Mara laughed. "Oh, why's that?"

"Because you're so pretty," said Katie, with a smile.

Mara stopped and put her hands on her hips.

"Me? Pretty? Nobody's ever told me that before."

"Well that's because everybody else is silly," replied Katie, quickly grabbing Mara's hand again.

That morning, Katie wanted Mara to explore the park with her. "And what about the other children? Your friend Lauren? And Esther? Can they come too?"

Katie shook her head. "No, just us two."

"And who's going to look after the other children here?"

"Janine can do that!"

But Janine — given the choice — didn't want to stay in

the playground. So in the end they all set off, in little groups rather than the usual single file. Cars weren't allowed in the park and there were separate cycle paths. It was safe for the children.

Mara hadn't known that there was a volleyball court in the park too. After all, she'd never been here before. She only knew the desolate park on the edge of her development in the south of the city, which was more of a neglected patch of grass, surrounded by stinging nettles.

That was where dealers met their clients in the evenings, where you found condoms in the bushes. The place where Dumpsters were crushed, their lids wrenched off their hinges. A godforsaken place.

But this park wasn't like that. Apart from anything else, it was bigger. With tall trees and alleys of rhododendrons, secluded viewpoints behind hedges of forsythia. A place where old people could go for a peaceful stroll and people in wheelchairs could rest by the pond and feed the ducks.

The volleyball court suddenly appeared in front of them. They had only been able to hear voices, cheers, and the occasional blast of a whistle.

They hadn't taken any further notice.

Katie was holding Mara's right hand and Lauren's left when a ball landed at their feet. And somebody shouted, "Can you throw it back, please?"

Mara picked the ball up and held it over her head. She was good at sports but she couldn't throw. If the ball came to her in a game and she was supposed to pass it, it was always likely to be embarrassing. Suddenly the bushes parted and a boy emerged. He was wearing Bermuda shorts and a polo shirt, and he froze as he recognized Mara. It was Tim.

"Hey!" He flung out his arms enthusiastically. "I don't believe it! Is it really you?"

Katie hastily grabbed Mara's hand. "Make him go away," she whispered.

"Why?" responded Mara.

"Because I want you to!" Katie stared resentfully at Tim as he came closer with a smile. "Go away, you silly boy!" she shouted suddenly.

Mara bent down and put her hand over Katie's mouth. "Stop it!" she whispered. "Stop shouting or I'll get mad!"

And Katie stopped at once. She let go of Mara, folded her arms, and pouted.

Mara looked around for Janine, who was behind her with the other children. She went a little way over to her and asked, "Will you look after Katie for a while? And the others, please! I'll be right back."

"No problem," Janine assured her. She looked curiously at the boy who had so suddenly appeared from the bushes. "Wow! He's cute!" she whispered. "Where do they make them like him?"

Mara realized that she was blushing.

"Okay," whispered Janine, giving her a friendly pinch on the arm, "I'll let you have him."

She nodded to Tim and walked on slowly. After a dozen or so feet, she stopped and explained something to the children, bent down, and pointed to a spot on the edge of the path: perhaps it was a rare plant, or a particularly pretty flower... But she couldn't keep the children's attention on it. The little ones kept glancing over to Mara and Tim, nudging one another and giggling.

Tim beamed when he and Mara were finally alone face to face.

"Hey, we've got a volleyball tournament here today. What a coincidence! What are you doing here with all those kids?"

She explained that she was doing a placement at the day-care center and Tim was enthusiastic.

"You like them, don't you?" he asked. He smiled at the children, who were still whispering and nudging one another. "The little girl was jealous just now, did you notice?" he asked.

"Katie's got a bit of a crush on me," she said.

Tim raised his hands. "Who hasn't?"

Mara couldn't think of anything to say to that.

"Honestly," said Tim, "I'd never have guessed that you'd be so good with children."

"See—you should never go by appearances."

"You're quite different from Sophie," said Tim. "It's really interesting. I always used to think that all girls were like my sister."

"What's your sister like, then?" asked Mara.

"Bitchy, vain, and TV-obsessed. I told you that she's got something on every afternoon, like me, but she spends the rest of the time either in front of the mirror or in front of the TV. Oh, and her other hobby is talking on the phone. She talks to her friends for hours and when you ask what it's about, she says, What? Does it always have to be about anything?" He shook his head apologetically. "The money my sister wastes on phone calls could feed a poor family for a month."

Mara didn't answer. She looked at him.

He was spinning the ball on his fingertip, probably to impress her. She had to smile, but Tim's trick attracted someone else's attention too. Suddenly little Katie, over on the path, broke away and appeared by their side and tried to ingratiate herself with Mara again by flinging her arms around her, pressing her head into her side, and staring wide-eyed at Tim.

"Hey," said Tim, giving her a gentle push, "there you are again. What's your name?"

"I'm not telling you."

"Her name is Katie," Mara informed him, "and she sticks like glue. Don't you?" She smiled and winked at the girl.

Katie stuck her little hand in Mara's again. "Come on," she said, "you promised that we'd explore the whole park."

Mara pushed her carefully away, but the little girl clung all the more fiercely. "Please come now. You promised." She was beginning to get on Mara's nerves.

"You want Mara all to yourself?" asked Tim cheerfully, tugging playfully on Katie's nose. She pulled a face and struck out at him, but it didn't bother him. He laughed good-naturedly. "It looks like you'd better go," he said, looking into Mara's eyes.

In any other circumstances, she'd have said, I don't have to do anything. I do what I want.

If something like this had happened at school, on the school grounds, if she'd been in the middle of a good conversation and the bell went, she'd have probably skipped the next class. Definitely for a boy like Tim. Although she'd never have done anything for a boy before.

But this was different. She was responsible for the kids and she was under a lot of pressure. That letter from Mrs. Sidler! Even if she had thrown it away in fury, it hadn't failed to have an effect. She knew that this time it was serious. If she left Katie here so she could go off alone with Tim, there'd be hell to pay—and she'd never need to show her face at school again.

Not that she was that bothered about school!

But hanging around at home? That was no better. When everything there was falling apart. When her mother... But she didn't want to think about that now.

"Okay," Mara took a deep breath and smiled at Katie, "shall we go back to the others?"

Katie beamed at Mara without taking her eyes off Tim.

"I've got the message," Tim exclaimed. "She belongs to you." He laughed again.

Mara hesitated. This had never happened to her before, that she'd been so bad at saying good-bye to someone.

"We're out of here," she said. "It's nearly lunchtime anyway. We've all got to go back."

At that moment, the cries from the other side of the bushes got louder. They were obviously getting impatient for their ball. Tim grinned. He dribbled the ball.

"Where is the day-care center?" he asked.

Mara gave him the address.

"And when do you finish?"

"At four."

"Okay, I don't know if I'll make it to meet you, I can't promise, but I'll try, okay?"

Mara nodded. Katie pulled her away as Mara saw Tim clutch the ball to his chest and force his way back through the leaves and branches to the volleyball court.

HE REALLY SHOWED UP. And he didn't wait in the courtyard, as Mara had imagined, he just came right in and stood there, beaming.

Normally there were a few stragglers. Sometimes she'd had to work an extra half-hour because some parent hadn't managed to arrive on time. But today everything went relatively smoothly. Just before four, there were only three children left, Carlos, Max, and Dennis; Max's father gave his son a piggyback and disappeared out with him into the hallway. Carlos was fighting with his big sister because he preferred to be picked up by Mommy, and Mara was just tying Dennis's shoes as Tim appeared in the doorway.

Janine, a mountain of toys in her arms, came out of the next room, stopped short, and grinned at Tim. "Oho, the volleyball player from the park! And—who are you picking up?" she asked.

Tim grinned back. He pointed to Mara. "That girl there."

Mara turned away quickly. The guy totally embarrasses me, she thought. How pathetic. But she was pleased too.

Janine pretended to stare in amazement. "Ooooh!" she stretched out the O for as long as possible. Then she passed really close to Mara and whispered, "He doesn't just look cute in sports clothes!" Mara didn't know where to look. But Janine was right.

His shoes tied, Dennis went outside to wait for his mother, perching himself on the edge of the playground, his teddy-bear backpack on his knees. I can't think where she's got to today, wondered Mara. She's not usually early, but she's normally here punctually when we close.

"We could play a game with him," suggested Tim, thinking of blind man's bluff or hunt the thimble, and Mara objected that nobody had played those games for fifty years, at which point Dennis's mother arrived, racing down the hallway with a glance at her watch. She apologized, explaining that most people turned up at the employment office where she worked just as it was about to close, then wondered why they were dealt with in a rush. "They've got nothing to do all day, but they still wait till day's end," she said wearily. She gave Dennis a hug.

Mara found herself thinking about her father. She could easily imagine that he hadn't got himself together to submit his claim for benefits until the afternoon. She didn't like the idea that he might have come across Dennis's mother and then abused her, blamed her for his problems.

24

TIM HAD TRAVELED ON his scooter; and he had a second helmet with him, which really belonged to his sister, Sophie.

"Where shall we go?" he asked. "Suggest something. I've got two hours."

"No idea," answered Mara. She had never been on a scooter before or worn a helmet, but she wasn't telling Tim that.

She acted cool. That was always safest.

"Hold on to me, okay?" Tim fastened the straps of his helmet under his chin.

She nodded.

"So? Where to? Do you have to go straight home?"

The idea of Tim dropping her off at the apartment made Mara feel totally sick. "Wherever you like. I've got plenty of time," she said.

It was a beautiful June day.

The scooter purred along and Mara enjoyed feeling the airstream.

They drove out to the lake. Black-and-white cows were trudging through a field of flowering milfoil.

Tim slowed down as they rode along the lakeside, where children were sailing remote-controlled boats.

Then an outdoor café appeared. Tim turned into the parking lot and stopped the engine.

"Damn, it's closed!" He glanced over to it, "I thought we could sit on the patio."

"We still can," Mara said, climbing off. The tables and benches were secured with chains, but they found two chairs that had been forgotten and sat down.

"I wanted to buy you a coffee," complained Tim. "And it's their day off. That's so stupid!"

"Doesn't matter," said Mara. "It's nice just like this."

It was true. They could hear the birds and the sounds of an open-air swimming pool in the distance. They hadn't been going to open it this summer because the city was almost bankrupt. But then the residents had protested so much that they'd opened it after all, a day or two ago. Mara didn't care. She couldn't afford a season pass. They must cost at least fifty dollars.

Tim told her all his favorite places, where he felt happiest. This lake was one of them, along with a spot in the countryside where his whole family went to pick blueberries. He knew one place where massive mushrooms grew, but he wouldn't let anyone in on the secret, not even his father, because when it came to mushrooming, they were rivals. In the winter, they went skiing.

"What about you?" he asked. "What nice places do you know?"

Mara thought about the commuter station where the junkies hung out, the McDonald's where she'd spent half the night, about her apartment block, about the alleys where homeless people slept in heaps of garbage. She couldn't think of any nice places.

She smiled in embarrassment. "Nice places? No idea. That's not really my thing."

"What do you mean that's not your thing?"

"Well. I mean, I don't run around ticking off the nice places in the city. Or thinking about where I'd feel happy."

Tim looked at her curiously. "Why not?"

Mara shrugged. "Dunno. I mean, everyone's different, aren't they?"

"Obviously," said Tim. "Everyone's different. But what are you like?"

"Can't you tell?" said Mara.

"No, I can't," replied Tim. "Do you know, I think you want to give the impression of being a punk. Someone who's always protesting. But I don't think that's what you're really like. I get that feeling. Because if you were like that, just saying to hell with the world, you wouldn't interest me at all."

"Aha," Mara kept acting totally cool. But she wasn't cool. It was strange to talk about herself with someone else. To hear someone else's thoughts about her. She could think of only one person who'd ever thought about her—considered what she could become: Mrs. Sidler. She didn't think that her parents had ever thought about her for a second. She was sure that she, Mara, was more worried about her parents than vice versa.

"So, are you a punk?" asked Tim. "I mean, is there punk in your soul?"

She looked at him. She saw the light in his eyes. Him watching her. She was wearing her black jeans with a matte-black T-shirt. She laughed. "Dunno. Maybe?" she looked around. There was a hawthorn bush at the end of the patio, swarming with butterflies. In the distance you could hear the quiet roar of the traffic on the road. There were white clouds floating across the sky. The dandelions were flowering in a meadow stretching behind the café, so yellow it hurt your eyes. She was wearing Velcro sneakers. When she looked at her sneakers, her feet began to glow. More than anything, she wanted to take off her sneakers and run barefoot through the dandelions. She tried to imagine what it would feel like to run barefoot through a bright, sunny meadow of dandelions.

Tim would run barefoot next to her, or no, they would lie in the grass and the soft dandelion petals would tickle their skin. They would lie on their backs and blink up into the sun and—

"What are you thinking?" asked Tim.

Mara looked up. "Do you really want to know?"

"Would I have asked if I didn't?"

"Okay then," said Mara. "I was thinking … " She smiled. "Damn. I've forgotten what it was."

"That's not true," said Tim.

There was no way that Mara could talk about what she'd

just been thinking. Like she could never talk about what people called feelings. She stretched her arms. She looked him straight in the eyes. She could be so cool, supercool.

"I always forget my thoughts. And my feelings."

"That's a shame," said Tim.

She shook her head. "No it isn't. It's practical."

He laughed skeptically. "What's practical about it?"

"If you forget your thoughts," she said, "you don't clutter up your brain with a load of crap. You never have nice thoughts anyway. It's mostly crap... Except occasionally... " She stood up next to her chair. She stretched her legs.

Tim got up too. "Do you often think crap?" he asked.

Mara bent down, opened the Velcro on her right shoe, and played with her toes, arched her feet.

"Thoughts are free, aren't they?" she asked. "Like in the old song. Do you know it?"

Tim nodded. "I think it means something else. But fine." He began to hum the song, forming the words quietly.

"Thoughts are free,

They cannot be guessed,

They flitter past like shadows to rest."

Mara couldn't take her eyes off him. She didn't care whether the song fit. It was amazing that Tim was singing for her. If only you could hold on to some moments. Like now. Stop the clock. That would be something...

"Give me your hand," Tim said.

Mara stretched her hand out to him, and he turned it over, studied the other side.

"Beautiful lifelines," he said. "Strong."

She wanted to pull her hand away, but he was holding it tight. He took a pen out of his pants pocket and began to write numbers on her palm.

"My cell number," he said. "Call me when you've remembered it."

"What?"

"Whatever you were thinking about just now"—he nodded toward the dandelion meadow—"when you were looking over there. You had a really beautiful look on your face then."

She laughed. She was embarrassed. She blushed. It wasn't easy to stay cool around a guy like this.

"We could go and get an ice cream in the city somewhere," said Tim, "and then I'll take you home."

Mara liked the idea of the ice cream, but not the taking home. She knew an ice cream place on her bus route, near an intersection. There was a bus stop nearby. She would get the bus. She'd think of an excuse. She could think of excuses standing on her head—there was no way that Tim could find out where she lived. Otherwise he might get the idea of turning up on her doorstep.

When she got back on the scooter, she stole a look at the cell number on her hand. She learned it by heart. Just in case the ink wiped off.

25

H ER MOTHER STILL HADN'T come back. She had disappeared without a trace.

She and her father had nothing to say to each other. It had always been difficult to be in the same room as her father, but now, today, after having such a good time with Tim, she just couldn't bear it.

And her room wasn't her room anymore. Somehow her mother had left her shadow behind in it. The smell of her depression, her anxiety, the revulsion. Something had happened to her room. Mara flung the window wide open and hung her sheets and duvet from the windowsill to air.

She cleared out her closet, just to kill time, stuffed everything she didn't need anymore into a large garbage bag. The television was on in the living room. Some lousy courtroom drama about people whose lives were just as crappy as the Dolans'.

Mara would have loved to go into the living room and say to her father, What are you watching that for? Watch your family instead—it's just like a bad TV show.

She wondered whether to go again, get out of here, wander around the city, as she usually did when it was unbearable at home. But she wasn't in the mood for that at the moment either.

She left her door open so she'd hear the telephone. When she was in the bathroom, she turned the tap on so gently that the water hardly made a sound as it ran into the sink.

She was afraid of missing the telephone if it rang.

Her mother was bound to call at some point. But the phone didn't ring.

She hadn't given Tim her number out of fear that her father might answer the telephone. And she was too nervous to phone him.

She wanted to keep cool toward him. He definitely expected that of her. He liked her because she was cool. Because she had punk in her soul...

No, she wouldn't call first. She would wait.

What was her mother doing? Why didn't her mother phone? She could at least try. See if it was working again.

Mara waited. Her father had managed to get the phone connected again, at least. He had been to the social services office and the official on duty had evidently believed that he, Gary Dolan, was in serious difficulties. If someone loses his job through no fault of his own, her father had explained, he wasn't in such a weak position. "They were sympathetic toward me and gave me a loan, interest-free, so I can pay off the outstanding bills. And I even got a coffee, from the machine. Tasted foul, but so what. Is there anything to eat?"

"I ate at the day-care," said Mara.

"My daughter, eating at a day-care center! I'm stuck with a little kid again!" grumbled her father. "Can the little kid fetch me a beer from the kitchen?"

"No," snapped Mara. "It can't. Get it yourself. Has Mom called yet?"

"She's not going to call now."

Mara started. She felt a twinge between her shoulder blades. It always hurt there when she felt suddenly afraid.

"Why won't she call now?"

"No idea. She's too glad to be rid of us."

"And where is she?"

"If I knew that . . . " Her father groaned and stood up. He had undone his pants to make more room for his stomach and be more comfortable. So he had to hold his pants up with both hands as he passed Mara. She heard the fridge door open and close again in the kitchen. The rich, sucking snap characteristic of fridge doors.

"What do you mean if I knew that?" shouted Mara.

"There's no more beer!" roared her father. He came back boiling with rage.

"I don't care about your friggin' beer! I want to know where Mom is!" Her father dropped onto the sofa again.

"She can't cope with anything," said her father scornfully. "You know what she's like, if you're a bit tough on her . . . "

Mara said nothing, just looked at her father, her eyes narrow. He did up his shirt and counted the change in his pants pockets.

"She thinks it'll be better somewhere else," he said. "She thinks she deserves a better life." He laughed bitterly. "What about me? Don't I deserve a better life? I'm the poor guy here! Me!" He thumped his chest with his fist. "And that goddamned neighbor," he said, shaking his fist threateningly at the wall, "if I find out that she's been sticking her nose in here again! Calling the police! What kind of country is this? This is still my apartment, I'm still the master in my own house!"

Mara took a step back. "The police?" she asked, startled. "They were here?"

"Damn right, they were here!" Her father laughed dryly. "Two patrol cars. Five officers. As if I was a dangerous criminal. I'm not mad! I wouldn't kill my own wife! She's not worth a life sentence!"

Mara shut her eyes.

"I need a drink," said her father. "Do what you like."

He picked up the key and went to the door. He opened it but turned back to her, pulled out his wallet, and leafed self-importantly through the bills. He pulled out a fifty.

"Housekeeping," he said proudly. "Buy something decent. Fill the fridge for a change. It's not like we're poor. I'll be off then." He pressed the bill into her hand and stroked her hair, somewhat clumsily but affectionately.

"It's just the two of us now, isn't it? We'll be all right."

"Where should I look for Mom?" Mara tried again. Her father shrugged, turned around, and left the apartment without a word.

26

ONCE HER FATHER LEFT, Mara felt worse rather than better. The silence that now reigned settled on her like dust.

But it wasn't just in their apartment that it was so quiet.

Normally you could hear the voices of neighbors, shouting, the TV in the apartment below, music, something. But there were other things missing too, such as the smell of other people's cooking, which crept under the door and showed you that you weren't alone ... Now the air smelled of nothing at all.

The cordless phone shone white on the sofa. She couldn't hold out any longer.

She knelt down next to the sofa, leaned against the cushions, and reached out to grab the telephone.

Slowly, thoughtfully, she dialed Tim's cell number.

"Hello? Tim Harris."

She could hear the roar of traffic, car horns, motors revving—as well as Tim's voice.

"Hello, it's me."

"Hello?" shouted Tim, "I can't hear you. Who is it?"

"Me."

"Who's me?"

"Thanks for the ice cream earlier, it was great."

He laughed. "Ah! Mara! Hey, calling already?"

She blushed. She looked at her watch. It was three hours since they'd seen each other, so surely it was okay to call by now?

"Are you busy?" she asked more coolly.

"I'm in the car with my mother. We're going to buy a new barbecue."

"Aha."

Mara tried to imagine Tim in the car with his mother, on the way to buy a new barbecue. She couldn't really picture it.

"We're in for some good weather," said Tim. "Loads of hot days. And we always have barbecues then. You know, real men are cowboys who throw meat onto the fire." He laughed boisterously.

"Pass it over."

Mara heard a female voice.

"My mom wants to speak to you. I'll hand you over."

Mara was startled. She ran her tongue over her dry lips. What should she say—?

"Hello? Mara?" she heard. "You're more than welcome, of course. We've got old friends coming this evening, but maybe at the end of the week? Or whenever you're free? We'd like to meet you."

She then gave the handset straight back. Mara stood there, paralyzed. She'd received an invitation! When was the last time she'd been invited anywhere? She could only remember a few birthday parties when she was little. She doesn't know anything about me, she thought. People don't do things like that. And since when have people had parties with their parents? What sort of weirdos are they?

"Hello?" yelled Tim. "Are you still there?"

"Yes."

"Sorry, Mom's so impulsive. Don't worry about it. But you're invited, I was just telling her about you. You see, it must have been something good. Mustn't it, Mom?" The question was aimed at his mother. Mara could only hear the noise of the car, she couldn't hear her answer.

"I've got to go," she said. "I just wanted to make sure I'd got the number right."

"Yep," said Tim.

"Will you be playing volleyball again tomorrow?"

"No. I've got French club tomorrow afternoon, it got moved. But will you be at the day-care again?"

"Sure."

"Okay, look out into the courtyard at four, perhaps I'll be there. Okay? Mom! We have to turn off here!—Hello? Hey, can you hear me? See you tomorrow..."

Mara hung up.

Tim was shopping with his mother. There was something so normal about that. Shopping with your mother. Planning something for the evening. Chatting to your mother, about school, about your friends. Your plans.

Suddenly Mara felt a lump in her throat. She swallowed.

It's strange, she thought. She'd been so angry with her

mother so often, because she wouldn't go to the doctor, because she'd let herself go so badly, didn't take care of herself, or Mara. But now she missed her and was scared for her. Scared that something could have happened to her, that she might...well, do something to herself...Goddammit! And as she thought, the rage rose up in her again.

I need a mother, thought Mara, but she's taken off. Left everything, abandoned it and gone.

Fantastic.

First my sister disappears and leaves me alone with Mom and Dad, then Mom disappears and leaves me alone with Dad.

But who knows, perhaps he won't come back from his pub crawl either.

She could feel her heart pounding. She ran into her room, scrabbled around in her desk.

Shit, she thought, what if I've thrown the paper away, if I haven't got Simone's number? I'll crack up!

When she visited, back in December, Simone had popped into her bedroom for a bit, to comfort her; Mara had been in floods of tears because her sister had refused to take her with her. But Simone had written a telephone number on the edge of a magazine article and said, "If anything happens, they'll always know how to get in touch with me. But only call if it's really urgent, okay? I don't want to bother these people."

She'd never called, although there'd been plenty of times in the last few months when she really could have done with Simone's help. She'd been too proud to phone. Or afraid that it wouldn't be the right time. She didn't want to be passed off or disappointed. Did Simone still love her? Would she stand by her?

As she hunted, she came across a heap of old notebooks that she no longer needed, a diary she'd started (when she'd been nine) and only written on two pages, old movie tickets, passes for the swimming pool, magazine articles about Britney Spears—she'd had a crush on her once—and finally she found, wedged into the back of the drawer, the folded article.

She went to the telephone and dialed the number.

She had to wait for ages but, just as she was about to hang up again, Simone answered, her sister was right there on the other end! Mara was so confused that she couldn't speak. Simone! It was really her! She hadn't heard her voice for six months. But wasn't this the phone number of some random people who'd always know where she was? Hadn't she said that Mara shouldn't bother these people by phoning unnecessarily?

"Hello! Who is it?" She cleared her throat. "Hello, Mona. Have I called you at home?"

Pause. Then more throat-clearing, an embarrassed cough.

"Maralise? Is that you?" Simone called her by her nickname straight away. She felt as if her body was warming up, as if she was relaxing. She almost smiled, just because she was touched.

"Yes, it's me. Hello, hey, where are you? Tell me!"

"Doesn't matter. You found me. Maralise! I'm glad you called!"

Does she really mean that? thought Mara. She waited. Simone, at the other end, was obviously waiting too. It's not so easy to break a long silence, Mara thought. And you both keep thinking during the silence, thoughts the other person doesn't know about. But Simone must realize something, of course. The feeling that something bad was happening. Had happened. The whole time.

"Mom's gone," said Mara.

More silence.

"Mom? Gone? What do you mean?"

"I mean, Mom's gone."

"Where is she?"

"I don't know, not a clue."

More silence.

"You mean, she might be on her way here?"

Mara hadn't thought of that. But it was possible. "Where are you?"

"Bellevue," said Simone. "You know that."

"No," said Mara. "I didn't know. I haven't got your address."

"I've always been in Bellevue. Nowhere else."

"Oh, right."

"So? What's up?"

Mara related the meager facts that she knew: their parents must have had a fight, Mrs. Vrabec, the neighbor, had called the police —

"When was that? Tell me from the beginning!"

Her sister didn't even know that their father had lost his job; Mara began again at the beginning. Then she told her about their mother's injury and her stay in the hospital.

"Mom had to go to hospital?" shouted Simone. "And you're only telling me now?"

Now she's finally getting worked up, thought Mara grimly, about time too.

"I don't know where to look for Mom. Or whether to go to the police, or what? Mona, everything here is totally shit!"

Suddenly she felt self-pity rise up inside her. The same as it did back when Simone gave her the telephone number. Perhaps her little sister's tears would melt Simone's hard heart?

But then Mara bit her lips and pulled herself together, so as not to cry. She lay back in the armchair, the phone wedged between her shoulder and her ear, and stared at the ceiling.

"I can't come," said Simone hesitantly. "I've got ... I'm in the middle of ... Well, I've got a few problems of my own here ..."

"With your job? Or what?"

"With everything," said Simone evasively. "But it doesn't matter. I don't want to talk about it."

Mara didn't ask anything else. Shame, she thought, after all, we're sisters. But she didn't say so.

"So, I can't leave here, it's impossible, but you've got to do something about it."

"Yeah, right," said Mara.

"Yes, hell! Perhaps something's happened to her! Call the police! They can tell you what to do!"

That possibility hadn't even occurred to her. Why not? Perhaps because of the cars the other day, when she'd... with her key. Or because of the chaos she'd caused in the supermarket. There must be something inside her, some kind of subconscious voice, saying, Watch it! Stay away from the police!

"And what about that Vrabec woman?" Simone was already making another suggestion. "Perhaps she knows something?"

She'd already thought of that. But it wasn't as simple as casually ringing the doorbell and asking, Do you happen to know where my mother is, by any chance?

"I could give you her telephone number," said Mara. "Couldn't you call her?"

She pulled the phone book over and opened it. V for Vrabec.

Simone laughed. "Hey, are you all there? Why should I phone your neighbor from Bellevue? Spend money on a phone call when you can ring the doorbell? Do you think I shit money?"

Mara didn't think that—if Simone did shit money, she might have stumped up a dollar now and then for her little sister.

"So, you can go over there now and ring the bell and say... "

"I know what to say. I thought you'd help me."

"Hey! What can I do?"

"Mona! She's your mother too!"

"Oh God! Don't take that attitude with me, okay? Of course she's my mother. But why should I drop my whole life now and ... "

157

Mara let Simone talk. She didn't contradict her, she didn't interrupt, she just listened. The words floated past her like flotsam on a river. She knew what her sister would say even before she said it. How lousy her childhood had been, how squalid her life had been, how weak her mother was, how unbearable her father was. She'd had to leave, she couldn't stand it anymore. Okay, so she, Maralise, had been left behind with their parents. But—

"Bye," said Mara, breaking into Simone's flood of words. "It's getting expensive. You can always phone if you want to know how it works out." She pressed the button, put the telephone down on the floor next to her, flung herself into the armchair, and wept.

An hour later she knocked on the neighbors' door.

27

"S OMEONE RANG THE BELL for ages," complained Mrs. Vrabec. "But I didn't know it was your mother. This building, there are too many crazy people. I don't open the door." She was holding her baby in her arms again. The child was thin and pale and had yellow gunk oozing from its eyes. "I was making little one clean. He had full diaper, right to top. I couldn't go to the door."

Mara looked at the baby. The woman said nothing.

"But I heard fight on stairs. That was your father who shouted. Like mad. And drunk. Threatened to your mother. She knocked, beat on door, here. Called for help. Like I told to police. But I, you know... the baby. And your father... so dangerous. Didn't want your father... not at all."

"I understand," said Mara.

The baby began to cry. Mrs. Vrabec stuck a soother in his mouth and looked at Mara. "And you don't know where... is mother?"

Mara shook her head.

"A friend, perhaps?"

"I don't think so. Perhaps once. But now... I've never seen one."

Mrs. Vrabec sighed. "Well, why should I know where is she? I can't know that!"

"I thought she might have said something to you."

"To me?" Mrs. Vrabec laughed. "Why me? We say hello when your mother puts out garbage bag. Always leaves it there. I'm always afraid, all the garbage..."

Mara had heard enough. From now on the neighbor would keep repeating the same old stuff. What use was that? She pointed to the child. "Your baby needs eyedrops. His eyes are infected."

"Really? How do you know?" Mrs. Vrabec looked at her baby in surprise.

Mara took the opportunity to disappear back into her own apartment.

She finally plucked up the courage to phone the police. It was all nonsense. What she'd done recently—they couldn't pin it on her—and the police officer that she got through to, Sabine Kinsey, was nice. Not that Mara would have thought that was possible.

The officer searched for the record of the incident. "Dolan, 178 Wilson Street." She was careful to ask Mara for her age and whether she was alone in the apartment and so on. Mara answered evasively. She didn't like being asked questions.

"I just want to know where my mother is," said Mara. "I can deal with the rest myself."

"Hasn't she called?"

"No."

"Then I'm afraid we can't do anything," she said. "According to this, your mother only said—this is what people in your building said in their statements—that she wanted to leave and never see her husband again."

"Oh, right," said Mara.

She was going to hang up but the police officer involved her in a long conversation about her home, her father, and all that, until Mara had said more than she'd meant to.

"Someone will look into it," said the officer in the end. "I'll pass the information on to social services. They'll be bound to send someone around. I don't know whether anyone will be able to come today—"

"Nobody needs to come!" Mara shouted vehemently. "I'll cope!" She was trembling when she hung up.

It was quiet in the apartment again.

If only Tim would call.

But he didn't.

She felt like she was in the aftermath of a natural disaster, an earthquake or a volcano eruption. Or as if an asteroid had collided with the planet. She felt alone, dreadfully alone. The silence meant she could hear the blood in her ears. It was a roaring, a buzzing, and it seemed to get louder. It deafened her, paralyzed her.

This numb feeling took hold of her and she felt it creeping into her heart. She found herself thinking about Mrs. Vrabec, who had said there were too many crazy people in the building.

I'm crazy too, thought Mara. I'm going crazy.

She opened the apartment door cautiously and stared out. She took a few steps barefoot without making any noise and listened on the stairs. But she could still hear nothing but the roaring in her head. Everything was full of silence. A paralyzing silence. Mara pulled herself back, let the door snap back into the latch, looked around in the apartment. Everything seemed strange to her. She seemed strange to herself. She clenched her fists and hammered on the wall.

"Mom! For God's sake! Don't leave me alone here!" she screamed.

She was startled by her shout and pressed her hand over her mouth and held her breath. Soon somebody'll come, she thought. Soon someone will complain or fetch the police again.

She looked for a clean glass, filled it with tap water, and sat on the sofa. She drank very slowly, a sip at a time, felt the water run down her throat, realized that she was calming down. Her outburst had cleared her head; the rushing in her ears was subsiding. She felt better now.

Outside it was getting dark. She stood up, went into the kitchen, opened the fridge, and found a package of dried fruit behind the open bottles of ketchup and jars of mustard and pickles. She went back to her room, made her bed on autopilot, eating banana chips and dried slices of apple, pear, and apricot.

Then she curled up under her duvet like a baby, felt for the light switch with one hand, and turned out the light.

I must think of something nice, the thought flashed through her head, otherwise I really will go crazy. She thought about Tim, about the barbecues that he and his parents were planning. She imagined a nice house with a big deck and steps leading down into the garden. Lawns beneath tall trees. Laburnum and lilac and rose bushes. And along the path, all her favorite flowers, poppies and delphiniums and clumps of daisies.

Tim smiled and turned the steaks over the coals with a skewer. His mother, a beautiful slim woman, came out of the house from the sitting room, where white curtains fluttered in the wind. She was carrying a pile of plates with a large bowl of salad on top. Mara was standing down on the lawn. Tim's mother called out to her, "Come and sit with us! There's room for everyone here!"

Then her alarm clock went off.

As she walked into the kitchen, still half asleep, to put the kettle on, the everyday noises of the building crowded in on her again. She found herself smiling. There was no trace of the deafness that had come over her so much the night before, or the numbness. She heard the hasty tread of feet on the stairs, the laughter of children, Mrs. Babadi's voice in the apartment below them, the radio in the Millers' apartment on the sixth floor, too loud as usual. It all sounded so familiar and peaceful. Perhaps this will be a better day, Mara thought as she brushed her teeth. After all, there has to be a better day sooner or later.

28

B UT IT BEGAN TO rain. Big drops splashed against the
window, and Mara couldn't find her raincoat. Her mood
worsened instantly. Cursing, she ran through the apartment,
waking her father (she hadn't heard what time he'd come
back the night before), who threw an empty water bottle at
her, and slammed the door. She realized that she'd forgotten
the "housekeeping." So what.

Down on the stairs, she met Mr. Newman, who was carrying a mop and bucket. He pointed to a dark stain outside
his apartment door. "Look at this mess!" he cried. "Someone
threw up outside my door! If I catch him!" He looked at her.
Mara dashed away.

The bus pulled away right under her nose and she knew
that there was no way she would make it on time. She wondered what would happen when she arrived late. Would Mrs.
Clement ring the school immediately? Or maybe she kept
some kind of points system? Would she then lose a couple
of points straight away?

The next bus finally arrived. It splashed up and Mara

boarded. She found an empty seat, probably the only one, and looked out the window, watching the smeary rain run down the glass and staring at the depressing gray outside.

There was bound to be trouble because she was late. Mrs. Clement would be angry with her, perhaps even pick on her. Like everyone else always picked on her and nobody helped her. Suddenly she thought that she could play hooky from the day-care too. Then she could walk around the shopping malls, where it was bright and dry and you could try out expensive cosmetics. She wondered whether she shouldn't just chuck everything in. The school would probably throw her out in any case. What good could Mrs. Sidler do by herself anyway? Whatever happened with the placement...

Just as she'd decided to get off at the next stop and take bus 26 instead, a fat woman took up position in front of her and spat, "Hey! How many times do I have to say that I want to sit down?"

Mara jumped. She hadn't heard a thing. "Here?" she asked in surprise.

"Yes! Unless you can see a free seat somewhere else?"

She looked around. The bus was still packed.

"When I was young, children would never have dared to deprive their elders of a seat!" said the woman.

"I'm not a child, and my life sucks," replied Mara.

"And how do you think I'm feeling?"

Mara looked at the woman standing in front of her. Her face was pale, pudgy, and bloated.

She was about to tell the woman what she thought of her, but then she remembered Rosa Riccione and what she was facing at school because of her, so she just hissed, "Okay, fine, you fat cow." The woman didn't hear her.

But Mara wasn't about to stand up straight away. She waited until the next stop. Let the old cow wait.

When she got to the day-care, she could hear the usual din from outside, from the courtyard, but inside things were even more hectic than usual. Mrs. Clement and Janine were stressed because one of the cooks hadn't turned up yet. "Just not coming in, without letting us know! I won't have it!" complained Mrs. Clement.

Janine was flitting between the kitchen and the main room, and she cast a desperate glance at Mara. Little Natalie had a coughing fit and spat her juice all across the table. Jin cried for his mommy. Ahmed tried to put his arms around him to comfort him but only succeeded in knocking Jin's chair over, and both boys fell onto the backs of their heads. Uproar. Mara picked them both up, comforted them, gave them each a kiss, wiped Jin's tears and praised Ahmed because, after all, he'd been trying to be kind.

Mrs. Clement came in wearing a raincoat. "I don't know whether Janine told you. On top of everything else, I've got to go to the dentist. I'm in terrible pain. You'll be all right without me for two hours, won't you?" She looked at Mara briefly but turned and left without waiting for an answer.

Janine and Mara cleared away the breakfast dishes, took the kids to the toilet, and supervised them as they brushed their teeth.

"What a bummer that it's raining." Janine pointed to the

window. "We can't go out. That would make things easier for us. In any case . . ." She didn't continue.

"In any case what?" asked Mara.

"You know," said Janine. "The DVD."

She'd forgotten all about that. Janine had ordered a DVD from the video store and it was ready for pickup today. It must be something extra special because Janine had been going on about it all week. She had wanted to arrange the schedule so that the children could take a detour, down the street where the video store was, on their way to the park today. Now that wouldn't work and the store was closing that afternoon for a couple of days. For inventory. From the look on Janine's face you'd think her entire life had gone down the toilet. She was so unpleasant that in the end Mara sent her off. "Just go. Go and get the damn thing before you drive us all mad," she said.

Janine hesitated. "You mean I can leave you here alone with everything?"

"It won't be all day, will it?"

"Of course not! I'll be back in an hour!"

Mara was sure she could manage the children alone for an hour.

"You'll have to keep them occupied," suggested Janine. "It would be best if you did some painting with them. They all like that."

"Okay," Mara nodded and turned to the children, clapped her hands, and shouted, "Shall we do some painting?"

Loud hoots as they all rushed to the cupboard for the painting supplies. They were wrangling over it instantly.

"Slowly! One at a time!" she pleaded. She laughed. She felt good. She would keep everything in order here all on her own, for an hour at least. She was needed, and Janine and Mrs. Clement were depending on her to get their "stuff" sorted, to go to the dentist and run an errand. She felt warm inside and her heart thumped.

"You're quite sure you'll be okay?" Janine was feeling a bit apprehensive now.

"Do I look like I can't cope?" asked Mara. It was intended to sound a bit harsh.

"Katie's having a bad day today." Janine pointed to the little girl. "Something's happened at home, no idea what. Her granddad brought her, but he didn't want to say anything. So don't overreact if Katie gets uptight."

Mara shrugged. One thing was certain: she'd have no problem with the little girl who was so fond of her. "If they were all as easy as Katie," she said, "it really would be great."

At that moment Katie turned around and looked at her. Deadly serious.

Mara went to her and pulled faces to make her laugh, but Katie's face didn't change.

Oh well, Mara would try it again later.

Janine disappeared into the cloakroom for fifteen minutes. When she reappeared, she'd let her hair down and brushed it until it lay on her back like a shining mass. She was wearing high-heeled sandals and had polished her toenails.

That's not for the sake of a DVD, thought Mara. That's for a guy. Did Janine have a crush on the young man who worked in the store? So long as she didn't stay away for longer than they'd agreed, she didn't care.

She and the children waved Janine off, and then Mara gathered the coloring paper and crayons, filled old yogurt containers with water, washed the paintbrushes, and put the watercolors on the table.

At first Katie kept chasing after Mara, then she snatched one child's drawing pad, tore another's paper, and snapped the last orange chalk. Katie really was unbearable today. She looked pale and had dark circles under her eyes.

When about five children were crying because Katie had teased them, Mara picked the girl up, carried her to the table, and sat her down roughly. "Fine, sit here and stay here," she said strictly.

Katie stared at her. It was quiet for a moment. Then she began to shout and hit out madly around her, her eyes shut.

Mara grabbed her wrist. "Stop it, Katie, please!" She was at a loss. "What's the matter with you today? What's happened?"

Katie was bawling. When little red-haired Anna came close to her, she kicked her away.

"Hey," warned Mara, "that's not nice. Do you hear me? We don't do that sort of thing!"

She picked Katie up and held her closely, with a vise-like grip, looking into her eyes. "Katie! Come on! What's wrong?"

She stopped bawling but wriggled in Mara's arms, bending back as far as she could. Then she shouted, "Go away! Go away! You're a stupid cow!"

Mara felt the blood rush to her head. She put the girl down again, slammed a drawing pad down in front of Katie, and grabbed an old coffee mug full of crayons. "Get drawing," she ordered.

"I want to paint! I'm not a baby!" shouted Katie, bawling again.

Mara didn't know what to do. Was it better to give in or to stick to her instructions? She decided on the latter.

"You can draw with crayons and that's that!" she decreed. "And not another word, got that?"

"I'm a big girl! I can do it!" shrieked Katie. "I don't want the stupid crayons!"

She picked up the mug and hurled it on the floor; it broke in two, the pencils clattering over the wooden floorboards.

Mara was fighting against her anger. "Pick the crayons up, now," she ordered Katie.

The girl leaned back, crossed her arms defiantly, and shook her head.

"Did you hear me?" spat Mara. She was getting angrier by the second. If she'd thought until then that being a kindergarten teacher was an easy job that you could do with one hand tied behind your back, she now realized it wasn't. She wanted to run out of the room, slamming the door behind her. She was angry and furious, but also hurt. Whatever had happened at home for the little girl—she couldn't understand how her behavior could change like this. For the last few days Katie had been so affectionate and loving and now she was the exact opposite: obstinate, awkward, and unbearable. What on earth could she do?

Katie crouched on her chair like a little devil, staring into space.

"If you don't pick up the crayons and the mug you broke right now, I'll shut you in the cupboard," announced Mara.

Katie said nothing, her arms crossed again, staring at the picture Ahmed was drawing, a picture of a lovely red car.

"Did you hear what I said?" Mara bent down, took her by the chin, and forced her to look into her eyes.

"I want paints!" Katie yelled into her face. Mara thought her eardrums would burst.

So she picked the girl up under her arms and carried her away from her chair. Katie hung like a sack of potatoes, making herself as heavy as possible, letting her feet drag along the floor.

Mara carried her to the cupboard, pushed aside the boxes of puzzles, and sat her inside it.

"When you want to behave again," she said, "let me know and I'll let you out."

Katie looked at her. Her breathing was rapid and shallow. She's upset, thought Mara. So am I. What a stupid, unequal battle.

"Do you want to behave?" asked Mara.

The girl shook her head. Her lips pressed firmly together.

Mara crouched down. She tried to make her voice gentle and coaxing, however wound up she was.

"What are you so angry about? Will you tell me? You can tell me anything, you know that."

Katie shook her head vehemently again. The tip of her nose shone pale. "Go away!" she shouted. "You're silly! I hate you!"

Mara slowly stood up again. Her eyes were swimming. She was astonished that a little girl could throw her off balance like this.

"Okay, have it your way!" she said, slamming the cupboard door shut.

The cupboard had a wooden door, the top part of which was decorated with fretwork.

She stuck a finger through one of the holes. "Hey? Katie?" she called.

The girl didn't make a sound.

Mara took a deep breath.

She turned around. And it was only now that she realized that the room was dead silent. All the children were staring at her. None of them was painting; they were all completely still.

She forced a laugh. "See? That's what happens when you're bad. Did you all see?"

The children nodded. Some of them shrank right back on their chairs, hunched in their shoulders.

"Don't worry," said Mara. "Katie's okay in there. Nothing can happen to her. So, what shall we do? More painting? Or play musical chairs?"

Silence. Nobody spoke.

She went to Jin, bent down and put her hands on his shoulder. "Do you know how to play?"

Jin shook his head without a word.

"Bobby?" she asked. "Do you?"

Bobby just turned away.

Mara asked Ahmed and Marian and Leila, and none of them knew the game.

"What?" she cried, making a determined effort to be cheerful. "Okay, I'll explain it to you..."

She began to arrange the chairs in a circle, the seats facing out. She looked for a cassette and explained that they should all run around the chairs, and they'd always be one chair short, and when the music stopped, everyone should sit down as quickly as possible. Whoever was last was out.

The children listened. They were still quiet, sneaking glances at the cupboard, but there wasn't a sound. It was dead quiet inside. And so they looked at Mara again and waited for the game to start.

Mara radiated cheerfulness, hopped around like a clown, pulled faces, spoke now with a squeaky voice, now with a gruff, bearlike one, and ingratiated herself with the children. The children squealed and laughed and nudged one another and giggled some more.

She wanted to prove that it was nothing to do with her that Katie was being troublesome, that it was entirely her own fault. If someone else couldn't get along with her, that wasn't her fault. She stroked Esther's hair, gave Bobby a kiss, kicked a ball around with Rebecca, and soon they'd all forgotten that Katie was sitting in the cupboard.

The game went well. The children had a great time. It was noisy, the chairs crashed, every time Mara stopped the music they all shrieked, and after a couple of minutes she could see nothing but heated shining faces.

"More! More!" shouted the children when at last the final chair had been removed and there was a clear winner. "Again!"

And so the game started again.

They shrieked with delight, the game was set up again, they all made for their places and the dance began from the top. Mara watched as she stood by the tape recorder, and then she remembered the day when she'd played, laughed, and fought like that. At home, in their apartment, when she was still a child.

She'd just started school. It was Simone's birthday and she was allowed to have a party at home, which was unheard of. Seven children were invited, and their mother had ordered an enormous cream cake, which tasted delicious.

Never before and never again was there such a party at the Dolans' home. They played musical chairs in the living room with a Michael Jackson CD, because Simone had a crush on him at the time. Mara had flitted around the line of chairs, quick as a flash, and had always been standing right next to a chair when the music stopped. She did it. Every time. She was already sitting down with a grin while the others raced to find a seat, pushing, shoving, and squeezing. Mara sat laughing on her chair. She won four times, the fifth time she lost. And was determined to play again. Because she wanted to win again and again, because winning was so great. Her mother had even thought of little prizes: bags of candy, pens, colorful pencil sharpeners, bars of chocolate. By the end of the day, Mara had won a bar of chocolate, a pen, and two pencil sharpeners, one of which she swapped for a box of gummy bears; she still had the other one.

She could see her mother now. She'd been to the hair-dressers especially for the party, and Mara remembered the big china jug of hot chocolate she had been allowed to carry from the kitchen to the living room. She hadn't spilled a drop. She'd been so proud. And Simone had beamed with joy. She'd had a party! They were all her guests! Now she'd be invited to other parties, and indeed she was.

They still had the china jug. But it wasn't ever used. Not anymore. They'd never had so many people around again...

Mara watched the children here, skipping around with red faces, hauling the chairs around, arguing or collapsing in laughing heaps on the floor, and thought about her own childhood. And she was totally amazed that she'd remembered something she'd completely forgotten: one happy day in her childhood.

SUDDENLY A RUSH OF warm air blasted into the room and, when Mara looked over to the door, Mrs. Clement was standing there. She was holding a compress to her cheek and looked wracked with pain.

Helplessly she raised her free hand and pointed to the tape recorder. Mara stopped the music at once. The children protested. They wanted to keep playing, but Mara called soothingly, "That's enough now, kids! Clear everything up. We'll play again another time!"

Mrs. Clement shut her eyes in torment as the chairs were dragged, squeaking loudly, across the floor. She approached. She looked around with a frown.

"Didn't Mrs. Larson come?" she asked.

Mrs. Larson, that was Olive, one of the two cooks. Natasha, the other one, had the day off today.

Mara shook her head.

"Oh God," groaned Mrs Clement, "what are we going to give the children to eat?"

She leaned against the wall and shut her eyes.

"The pain must be very bad," said Mara sympathetically.

"He had to extract the tooth, a molar. There were complications because the root was so strong. My head is pounding."

"Wouldn't you rather go home? And lie down?" suggested Mara. "I'm doing all right." She indicated the children. "They're having fun."

"Yes, I can see that. Good." The kindergarten teacher looked at the children and frowned suddenly. "Where's Janine?"

Mara had to admit that Janine had just popped out for an hour, to run an errand. Mara avoided the words "video store." She realized that that wouldn't be well received. But it wasn't well received in any case.

"Janine left you here alone with the children?" she asked in bewilderment. "Doesn't she know that you're only a work experience student? Oh God, what if something had happened!"

At that moment they heard a whimper, a piteous little cry.

Mrs. Clement, still holding the compress to her cheek, dropped her hand. She looked around in shock. "What was that? Did you hear it?"

Mara felt as though her heart had skipped a beat, then it began to hammer in her throat. She had forgotten about Katie in the cupboard! Totally forgotten her! She should have let the girl out ages ago. The crying got louder. Mara felt feverish. She felt burning hot all over. The blood rushed to her head.

What should she do now?

"I know what it is," she said hastily. "I'll take care of it. Do you want a cup of tea?"

"No, I don't want tea!" snapped the teacher. She'd become suspicious. She listened. The crying had turned into sobbing. "Who is that?" she asked. "I know that voice. Katie?"

Then Katie began bawling her eyes out with long, drawn-out howls, like a little wolf.

Mrs. Clement went as pale as chalk. "Where is she?" she whispered.

"In the cupboard." Mara said it so quietly that Mrs. Clement couldn't hear.

She went to the cupboard, and the moment she door opened, Katie fell toward them, surrounded by dozens of boxes of games and puzzles. Some of the lids came off and all the little pieces scattered across the floor.

"For God's sake!" Mrs. Clement raced to the girl, knelt next to her, turned her on her back. Katie's eyes were clenched shut. Her face was stained with tears and she had wet her pants.

The teacher took it all in with one glance, the child, the open cupboard door, the torn-up puzzles and shredded box-es—Katie had evidently taken her fury out in destruction for quite a while and perhaps not even cried, maybe even enjoyed her desperate defiance. And so she'd simply been forgotten.

"Shut... in... the cupboard?" Mrs. Clement emphasized every word. She was staring at Mara as if she were a strange animal in a zoo.

Mara sank her head. She knew that the teacher was waiting for some kind of explanation. But what should she say? Her mind was a complete blank.

Katie turned on her side, put her hands over her face. Mara saw that the girl was stealing glances at her from between her fingers. She's okay, she thought. She's milking it.

She felt relieved, but the relief was no real help.

"You shut a child in a cupboard?" repeated Mrs. Clement.

Mara, her head bowed, said nothing.

The teacher bent over Katie, picked her up, covered her face with kisses, while groaning because it hurt her jaw, and whispered, "I'm so sorry, sweetie. Oh God, oh my goodness. I've never heard of such a thing..."

Katie began sobbing again; she clung to Mrs. Clement like a little trembling monkey who'd nearly lost her mother. "I want my mommy!" she whimpered. "I want to go home! Where's my mommy?"

"Soon, sweetheart, we'll call your mommy soon."

"No! Now!"

Mrs. Clement held Katie in her arms and looked accusingly at Mara.

"I'm sorry," said Mara. "I... was so angry... The kid was out of control. I wanted... only for a moment..."

"You're sorry? Is that it?"

What else could she say? How could she explain?

"It's…" Mara stuttered, "I mean…nothing can happen in the cupboard—my father used to…" She hesitated. She smiled at Katie.

"Shall I get you some clean pants?" She stretched out her hands. But when Katie saw that Mara wanted to touch her, she dissolved in tears again.

Mara dropped her arms helplessly. Mrs. Clement comforted the child. The others were standing around in amazement. They were even quieter than before. They were watching Katie with a mixture of curiosity, sympathy, and horror.

"Get your things and go," said the teacher quietly. "Right now."

Mara didn't move.

"Now?" she said, as if she hadn't understood. "Go now?"

"What do you think?" responded Mrs. Clement. "Did you think I'd just…? Oh no, I don't know what to say. Just go."

"But I… it's… Mrs Sidler said…"

Mrs. Clement lowered little Katie carefully to the floor. "I don't care what your teacher says or thinks. I don't want to see you here again. You're completely unsuited to our work here. Don't you realize that? Why are you still standing there?"

Mara said nothing. She bowed her head again.

She thought about Mrs. Clement phoning Mrs. Sidler and telling her all that, about it being noted in her school records. Mara shut a little kid in the cupboard! She's a monster. She's dangerous. She's shown that she's not capable of developing the least bit of social responsibility. Let her sit around alone in the apartment with her father forever. It would have been better if she'd never been born, never come into the world . . .

Mara plunged out.

Her thoughts and the voices were whirling around her head. She could hear her classmates' laughter, the teachers loving every minute, and saw Mrs. Sidler's eyes fixed on her.

She ran.

She didn't notice the rain. She didn't notice that she was running through puddles or that the water was splashing on her pant legs. She ran people over, barged into a stroller, and—accidentally—knocked over the newspaper stand by a kiosk. The stallholder yelled something after her. She just stuck her finger up at him as she ran. Kept running.

A new thought took hold of her.

Tim is coming to meet me at the day-care at four, she thought. At four. Bummer that I forgot Dad's money this morning. Otherwise I could have phoned him right away. I've got to get in touch with Tim.

As she turned onto another road, she suddenly noticed that a car was keeping pace with her.

For a while she took no notice of it because of the roaring in her head and the blood pounding at her temples, but then, when the car drove through a puddle and she had to jump aside, she did look at it.

It was Albert Droste, the caretaker. Wearing his mirrored sunglasses as usual, with his poser jacket over his open shirt. Two signet rings. His hands on the leather steering wheel.

Yellow leather seats. His sports car. He'd rolled down the passenger window.

Mara slowed her pace, dropped to a walk, and finally stopped, panting. Then she noticed for the first time that she couldn't get her breath back and that she had a horrendous stitch. Breathing hard, she stared at Droste.

"Look who we've got here!" he called.

She ran her hands over her head, her hair was dripping wet. She was dripping wet all over. But it had stopped raining. She looked up to the sky and observed that the clouds were dispersing, that a patch of blue could be seen again. She hadn't even noticed that it was no longer pelting down.

The sports car, like a silvery fish, gleamed suddenly as a ray of light struck it. She stared at it and thought, Lousy gloater car. Lousy Droste, fuck off.

He opened the car door from inside. "I'll give you a lift," he said.

She slammed the door shut again. "Fuck off," she murmured. But he didn't react. He bent over the empty passenger seat and smiled.

"Prickly, aren't you?" he asked with a grin.

Mara was fuming. This was all she needed.

She gave the car a kick. Nothing happened; her white sneakers were no use as a weapon.

"Hey!" cried Droste. "Are you crazy?"

"Fuck off!" she was shouting now. "Don't you get it? I don't want to talk to you."

Droste switched off the engine and jumped out of the car. In two steps he was by her side, holding her firmly by the arm. "Oh no, babe, oh no," he breathed. "When I speak nicely to you, the least you can do is be nice back. Don't forget who I am. Get in now. I'm not messing around. I'll take you home. Or what do you think?"

Mara didn't struggle as he opened the passenger door. She didn't want a scene. Especially not today.

Opposite them, across the road, was the movie theater she always went to. Next to it was the parking lot and, farther to the right, the footbridge to the commuter station. As usual, there were groups of teenagers hanging around outside the theater. A few of them were sitting on the steps, which were still wet from the rain, idly flicking their cigarette butts in the oily puddles. Two girls in miniskirts, heavily made up, were perched on the edge of the fountain, trailing their arms in the water. A couple were making out openly, as if they were alone in the world.

A couple of boys from her school were leaning against the wall with the film posters. Mara didn't know whether they were more interested by the flashy car or by her argument with the driver. They'll be calling me a whore again, she thought, saying I've got a pimp who drives a sports car. Who cares, let them think what they like. No scenes... And it wasn't exactly fun to wait for the next bus when she was wet through like this.

Mara flopped into the leather seat and Droste shut the door. He walked around the car, got in, and started the engine. "Okay then," he said with satisfaction. "Let's go."

Mara said nothing and stared out the passenger window. Droste slipped into the moving traffic.

"I didn't even recognize you at first," he said. "I just saw a long-legged gazelle running. You've got a good rhythm, I must say. I know a little about it. I always wanted to run a marathon. There's something automatic about your movements, you know? You run like someone who isn't thinking about running. They're always the best."

"Do you always talk such shit?" asked Mara. She was perfectly well aware that she was a good runner. He could stuff his flattery.

He laughed. He didn't care whether Mara was friendly. He'd never known her to be anything other than bad-tempered.

Droste didn't even wait for the next traffic lights before putting his hand on her knee. Mara jumped and slid away from him. Of course, she should have known that he'd be quicker to take advantage when he'd got her alone in his car than on the sidewalk outside the apartment block. But she'd get through this. The main thing was that she'd soon be home.

"How's your family?" he asked, playing the innocent. "I haven't seen your father for a while."

"Yeah, okay," Mara answered monotonously.

He changed up a gear and let the engine roar, glancing across at her as if to check whether she was impressed by this demonstration. Mara's expression didn't change.

"It's just that I still haven't had the rent," said Droste, "I often used to meet your father in the morning on his way to work. Is he ill?"

Reluctantly, Mara informed him that her father had lost his job.

"Oh." Droste shook his head in concern. "That's bad." He braked because a cyclist wanted to turn off ahead of him and there was a truck coming toward them. "Very bad. Is he getting welfare now or what?"

"Yes," said Mara. "What else?"

Droste nodded, then he sighed significantly.

"But that won't be enough, do you realize that? Never mind the fact that there's so much to make up." He sighed and shook his head concernedly again. "That isn't enough to pay for an apartment like that. I mean, I know it's not the best area in the world, but it's better than being on the streets, isn't it?"

He grabbed her knee again, his hand wandered farther up her leg. Mara hit his fingers. "Stop that!" Droste laughed.

"I'm hot for you, you know that! And do you know what I like best about you? That you're so obstinate. I could have any woman, I hope you realize that."

Mara didn't react. It was best to let him drivel.

"I've got a sports car, a penthouse apartment with a Jacuzzi, and good looks."

Mara looked out the window, deliberately bored. Droste wouldn't shut up. "Or don't you think I'm good-looking?"

"I've never thought about it," Mara muttered. She avoided looking at him. Just thinking about his chest hair made her sick.

Droste was in a good mood. He obviously didn't care what she thought, he was acting the part of a cheery soul.

Suddenly he turned right. This wasn't the way back to

184

the apartments. What was he doing? She felt a pressure in her ears, pounding on her eardrums.

"Where are you going?" asked Mara, trying to read the street signs. Droste raced into the fast lane at 125 miles an hour, flashing past all the slower cars on the right. Perhaps he just wanted to impress her with his car again.

"Just for a little spin," said Droste cheerily. "I'll take you back home soon enough, don't worry. It's fun in a sporty little number like this though, isn't it?"

Mara thought about needing to phone Tim. "I want to go home," she said. "I only got in because you . . ."

Droste wasn't even listening. He kept on boasting.

"Women don't want beginners in bed. Women want a guy who knows how to look after them. Razzle-dazzle, you get me?" He drummed like mad on the steering wheel. "I could tell you stories about girls your age that were already crafty little minxes." He laughed to himself and looked sidelong at her.

Mara felt her cheeks; she pressed her lips together and said nothing.

After a while, Droste picked up the thread again. "I can have who I want, when I want, how I want, and for as long as I want."

He stepped on the brake: a minibus had pulled out in front of them. After the speed they'd been doing, it felt like a snail's pace.

Mara wondered whether this was the moment to jump out of the car. They were passing a rest stop where an extended family was having a picnic. There was an enormous cooler next to the benches. The father had a massive pita bread in his hand. The mother was giving out things to eat. She had a headscarf on.

"I've been watching you for a while," explained Droste. "I've always had my eye on you. You were only little, you didn't have any ti…"—he grinned and corrected himself—"any breasts, but I wanted you back then. There was something about you…"

Mara moved farther away. Strangely, she wasn't afraid. She just felt revolted. And she kept thinking about Tim.

Then she saw the sign: Motel 3 miles.

Droste was drumming on the steering wheel again.

"But I waited," he said. "I watched you and waited until you were ready, you know?"

Mara reached for the door handle. She wondered what would happen if she just pulled it now. Would she manage it? At this speed? Was there too much wind resistance?

"If I'd seen you messing around with some boy, someone else pawing at you," said Droste, "I'd have acted before now, obviously. But there wasn't anyone, was there?"

She didn't answer. Her heart was in her mouth and she was suddenly close to tears. Just don't cry, she told herself, just don't cry, he might like that, and she swallowed the tears down.

Droste laughed. "I know there wasn't anyone, I know you."

Another sign. Motel 2 miles.

Droste took his foot off the gas.

"The crazy thing is," he said, "that I was already in the

mood for a little adventure when I met you. Where did you spring from, anyway?"

That was the first time that Mara had thought about the day-care center since she'd been in the car. About Katie. About Mrs. Clement. She hadn't even seen Janine again, had run away before she'd come back from the video store. Mara wondered briefly whether Mrs. Clement would throw Janine out too.

Perhaps Mrs. Sidler knew already? Was she sitting in the staff room writing another of those letters: . . . you know I've always stuck up for you, but I'm so disappointed in you . . . enough is enough. Mara, you must leave the school.

Motel 1 mile.

Droste pointed to the sign. "That's a good joint," he said. "They've got a really nice bar. I'm thirsty. We could have a drink."

He had to decrease his speed again before the exit. Surreptitiously and as carefully as possible, Mara pulled on the door handle. But Droste still saw it.

"Central locking," he said cheerfully.

He pointed to a button. "When I press that, all the doors are locked. It's a security measure, you see? So nobody falls out." He grinned. "And to stop gangsters from opening the door from outside and doing anything stupid. The likes of us aren't safe in this country anymore. It's all going to hell."

Mara shrank back in her seat. Now she started to feel something like fear. She saw the fleshy paws of the man at the steering wheel. The guy was strong.

She would have to see what happened. She'd have to wait for an opportunity.

Droste drove into the parking lot. They got out. Mara looked around. A large green area, a few trucks, two exits, both leading to the highway. She waited next to the car while Droste locked up. He smiled. He came around, put his arm round her for a second, and then slowly walked her over to the motel entrance.

"We'll have a drink," he said, "and chat for a while. Okay? I promise not to say another word about your parents. In any case"—his tone changed, became serious—"we won't need to speak about the rent and ugly things like that anymore . . . Depending on you . . . Okay? What do you think?"

Her face didn't change.

They went into the motel entrance. Pale blue armchairs and a Formica counter, with a woman sitting behind it, looking after the room keys.

"Hello, Evie," said Droste cheerfully. "Not busy today?"

The woman raised her head; she was in the middle of a crossword puzzle. She beamed as she saw Mara's "companion."

"Nah," she said, "it's always pretty grim when the boat show's over."

Mara knew that it was a tradeshow for boat owners, well-heeled types.

Evie didn't even glance at her, just turned around and looked at the wall with all the keys.

"Same room as usual?"

"The best," said Droste.

The woman put the key on the counter and he reached out for it. "It's always the best," she said.

Droste pulled Mara, who was standing motionless next to him, closer. "The kid's worth it," he said. "She's a real sweetie. I've been looking forward to her for a long time."

The woman grinned suggestively from behind her counter and bent over her crossword again.

Droste turned toward the hallway leading to the rooms.

"I thought we were going to the bar," Mara had a sudden inspiration.

He laughed. "Sure, okay, sure. There'll be a fridge upstairs too, though."

"I'd rather stop here first," said Mara.

He didn't like that, she could tell. But he wanted her to stay compliant... He led her to the bar. A pair of lovers was sitting in the dimmest corner; the woman had a very short skirt. The man had his hand between her legs. There were two men leaning at the bar, drinking beer and talking business. At the far end crouched another man, who was the same age as Mara's father and looked similar. He was drinking vodka.

She and Droste settled in a cluster of black faux-leather chairs. He ordered a gin and tonic for himself. Mara wanted a Coke—and to know where the toilets were.

Droste looked at her suspiciously. "There's a super bathroom upstairs," he said. "You can use that and have a shower or a proper bubble bath. Afterward too, if you want."

Mara didn't answer.

He didn't want to let her go, he was afraid that she'd run away. "I won't run away," she answered with a smile.

Droste looked at her. Then he grinned, leaned back, and spread out his arms. His chest shone with the golden chain and the tufts of hair. "Why should you," he said. "You're horny too. I can tell."

Mara stood up, walked out, past the washrooms and back into the entrance. That Evie was still sitting over her crossword.

"I need to use the phone," said Mara.

"Is that going on the bill?"

"Of course," she answered.

The woman pointed to a phone booth. "Dial 2, wait for the tone, and then dial the number."

Mara closed the door firmly behind her. She pressed Tim's number on the keypad. She looked at the clock, it was 1:30 p.m. If she was lucky, Tim would have just got back from school before his French club.

She let it ring for a long time. Just as she was about to hang up, someone answered: "Yes? Hello?"

It was Tim's mother. On his cell phone! Mara was so surprised that it was a while before she could get a sound out.

"Hello," called Mrs. Harris, "can I help you? Who's there?"

Mara cleared her throat. "I . . . uh . . . hello, this is Mara. I don't know if you —"

"Of course I do! Mara! Of course!" His mother was friendly. "You want to speak to Tim, don't you?"

"If I can." Mara was uncertain.

"'Fraid not. Sorry. He left his cell phone behind at home. Left it on the breakfast table this morning." She laughed. "These boys are always texting each other the answers to their math questions before the class. And that's before they spend the whole afternoon chatting on the Internet... Are you a web-freak too?"

"I haven't got a cell phone," said Mara, "or a computer."

"Very sensible," said Tim's mother. "Gives you more time for other things."

If you knew, Mara thought, where I am right now, what I'm doing here, very sensible... She felt really dizzy as she thought about Droste waiting for her at the bar.

"Tim's got some club or other. French, I think. Shall I give him a message? I'd be glad to. I'm always on his cell phone anyway. Not that it gets me anywhere."

Leave it then, thought Mara. It's not your phone. It's none of your business who your son phones. Or who phones him... Apart from the fact that everything at home was wrecked and crushed underfoot—she couldn't imagine family life where the parents always knew what their son—or daughter—was doing, who he was meeting or who he'd fallen for.

"Mara?"

She hesitated. Mrs. Harris had asked if she could take a message. "Yes, perhaps. We were going to meet this afternoon; he was going to meet me at the day-care."

"Oh yes! The day-care! He told me that! You're doing a placement there, aren't you? I'm glad. I love children too."

Mara scratched her fingernail along the phone box. She wouldn't say anything on that subject. She didn't ever want to think about the day-care center again, wanted to wipe it from her life. Rub it out. That would be best.

"But I'm not there," said Mara hastily. "I wanted to arrange to meet somewhere else instead. I mean, could you tell him not to go to the day-care?"

"Certainly, if I see him first. I'll leave him a note, but I don't think he's coming home for lunch. When he's got French club in the afternoon, the boys always go to the bistro with their tutor."

Mara thanked her, wished them a nice evening, and hung up.

She hoped it would work. Perhaps Tim would come home first anyway, or the French club would run late. She had done what she could.

And now to get out of here.

Droste was sipping at his gin and tonic and looking at his watch.

"I've changed my mind," she said. "You'll have to go up to the room alone. I'm not coming."

Droste put down his glass. He stared as if he'd misheard her. "What?" he said with a frown.

"I don't care whether you throw us out of the apartment," said Mara. "And I care even less how many other women you've had here. Or whether there's a super bathroom. I'm not doing it, not today or ever. Got it?"

Droste stood up slowly. He looked around surreptitiously. Nobody was watching them. He grabbed her wrist. He was rough.

"You miserable little rat," he hissed. "Why did you come with me then?"

"Aren't you getting confused?" asked Mara. "You were going to take me home!"

"I'm not letting you go that easily," he said.

Mara turned her hand, and it hurt as her skin was squeezed. But she got free. She simply turned and left the bar. He dashed after her.

The barman called out, "Excuse me! You haven't paid!"

Droste stopped behind her. He couldn't just walk out of here like that. After all, it was his "local." She heard a few coins clatter onto the table and then his hasty steps. Mara began to run. She pushed open the glass doors and was out in the parking lot. She looked round.

Droste had already grabbed her.

"Oh no," he hissed. "Oh no, my pretty."

All the friendliness had disappeared from his face. "Albert Droste isn't going to be messed around by a slut like you."

Mara pulled herself free, looked him in the eyes. She had that look again. She knew it, she could feel it. And the strength that came with rage, with anger. She waited. Quite coolly. A second, another second.

And then she kicked. Kicked him once in the stomach. Droste stumbled back; she followed it up with a second kick. Lower down this time. The man's eyes goggled, his mouth opened, his face was contorted with pain. He crumpled up and pressed his hands between his legs.

She turned and ran.

He didn't know how good she was. How hard she trained, he had no idea. He thought she was one of those willing little girls. Had he really thought that? That he could get her that easily? That he could do what he liked with her?

Okay, she'd blown it at the day-care and she'd be expelled. And her mother had gone. Fine.

But that was no reason for a guy like Albert Droste to think he could treat her like shit.

A truck started up behind her in the parking lot and drove toward the exit. Mara raced over the lawn to catch it. She raised her arms, gesticulated wildly.

The truck stopped. The passenger door opened, a boy of about fifteen looked at her curiously.

"Can you give me a lift?" Mara panted.

The boy turned to his father, who regarded Mara thoughtfully.

"Back. Just into the city." Mara pointed to the west. From the parking lot you could see two giant cooling towers with clouds of white steam.

"All right then," said the driver. "You're in luck, that's where we're going. Shove over, son, let her in."

When she turned her head she could see Droste, still crumpled up with pain.

29

WHILE SHE WAS FISHING around for her door key, she heard the telephone.

Tim! she thought. But no, he didn't have her number. Perhaps it was her mother?

It carried on ringing while she blundered around the apartment, hunting for the handset. But when she eventually found it, in the kitchen, and answered, it had gone dead.

Mara sat at the kitchen table and dialed Tim's cell number.

She let it ring a long time and then his voicemail cut in. First some music, reggae, then his voice, relaxed and care-free: "Hey, people, you're right. This is Tim Harris's phone. Say what you wanted to say and I might call you back."

I might! Hey, people! Say what you wanted to say!

She said nothing. She was silent for a moment, breathing audibly. Breathe in, hold, breathe out. Now he could wonder who it was. Then she disconnected.

It wasn't until she'd put the phone back on the table that she realized how stupid she'd been. Why hadn't she left him a message? He'd obviously not gone home, and his mother wasn't there either. He could listen to what she said later. If he hadn't gone to the day-care center after all...

She cleared her throat a couple of times so her voice wouldn't sound rough and strange, redialed his number, and waited for the voicemail. Then she said, "Hello, it's me. Um, I just wanted to say that I left the day-care early today. If you want, you can call me, I'm at home. My number is..." She gave him the number and ended her message.

It wasn't until she was in the bathroom that she realized that it had been a mistake to tell him the number. What if he phoned and her father answered! When he'd been drinking! And muttered or swore into the receiver, like he often did.

But it was done now. And she would have to expect him to call here at any time.

After all, that was what she wanted. For him to call, to hear his voice.

The only voice that made her feel good. And warm. The only voice that made her happy.

While she was still in the bathroom, the phone rang again. It was Janine, from the day-care.

"Hey, d'you know how often I've phoned? Why haven't you been answering?" she shrieked. "What were you thinking? You shut Katie in the cupboard while I was out?"

Mara kept silent for a second, to give her a moment to prepare for what was coming. She closed her eyes. "Janine, please," she said, "you've got to believe me... it was only meant to be for a few minutes... then I forgot... It was a mistake."

"A mistake!" Janine laughed hysterically. "How can something like that happen by mistake? Did you do it to get back at me?"

"What for?" Mara didn't understand.

"Because I left you alone with the kids?"

"That's bullshit."

"Well, it's caused me loads of stress," whined Janine. "And Katie's mother went ballistic. Mrs. Clement said we had to tell her because otherwise she might find out about it from Katie. And you can imagine what would have happened then . . . God! You must be insane!"

She let Janine's words wash over her. She said nothing. She crouched against the wall, her knees pulled up.

"Mara? Are you still there?"

"Of course I'm still here."

Janine changed her tone.

"Good, okay, the other reason I'm calling is that I've got a message for you, from your guy."

Mara raised her head. Coincidence or not, at that precise moment, a narrow shaft of sunlight shone through the little kitchen window onto the opposite wall. Like everywhere else in the apartment, she'd pushed the curtains aside, two narrow scarves.

"Really, and?" Mara's voice was hoarse.

"What's his name again, Tim? He called the day-care. He sounds as cute as he looks. He's really fun."

Thank you, she thought. Get on with it. Tell me what he wanted.

"I didn't tell him anything about the incident with Katie, by the way. I was that kind. I just said you'd gone home early. Which was true. I didn't have to say why, did I?"

"What did he say?"

"That he's busy today. I don't know, were you supposed to meet up? Was he picking you up?"

Mara shut her eyes and ran her hand over her brow.

"Mara? Then he said something else."

"And? Get on with it."

"Um, that he can't do tomorrow either. He's got something on with his family. Getting new furniture or something. Anyway, he can't come."

"Okay."

"Crap, isn't it? You like him."

"It's okay," said Mara. "I'm probably... busy tomorrow anyway."

"He wanted your number, but I couldn't remember where we'd put it and I didn't want to ask Mrs. Clement. As you can imagine..."

Janine chattered on for a while about the stress she was having at the day-care now, but Mara wasn't listening. Eventually Janine hung up.

Mara sat like that for a long time, her head on her knees, her legs drawn up, staring into space.

She wondered where Tim was right now. Where he'd called from if he'd left his cell phone at home. Okay, he could have borrowed one, but she was somehow suspicious.

The French club today was believable all right. But furniture tomorrow? What was all that about? No, he just didn't want to see her. He wasn't in the mood. He'd got better things to do. No wonder. She could think of better things herself. Why would he want to see a girl who shut kids in cupboards and knew gross men like Droste, who'd nearly got her into a hotel room? A girl who always lost it, got into fights, who didn't even have a proper family. There was definitely better. She felt so bad, so ugly, so excluded...

There was a knock on the door. Mara didn't react. The knocking got louder and someone called out.

It took a while before she realized it was Mrs. Vrabec.

She got up with an effort, shuffled into the hallway, and opened the door.

Mrs. Vrabec was wearing a dressing gown and had a towel round her head. She had makeup on. She smiled. She tried to squint past her, through the gap in the door into the apartment. But Mara only opened it a crack, so there was hardly anything to see.

Her neighbor rolled her eyes expressively, came right up close to her and whispered, "I had a call. Is he there...?" Again, she tried to peer in.

"Do you mean my father?" asked Mara, then shook her head no.

Mrs. Vrabec smiled. "Good. I should only say to you, not him. She said so. Your mother."

Her mother had called.

Thank God, finally a sign of life. Mara had been longing for it so badly: her heart pounded; she almost felt dizzy.

Mrs. Vrabec fished a little slip of paper from her dressing gown pocket and handed it to her. "That is address. 189

Charlesworth." She kept her voice down, looking round toward the stairs, as if someone might overhear her from there. "She is with colleague," she whispered, "from before."

"What's her name?"

"What it says. Kathy Wroblevski. Or something like that, you will find it."

"And what should I do?"

"What else? Go there! Speak with your mother! She say you something, I think. Perhaps she need your help. But not tell your father."

"I wouldn't anyway," growled Mara.

"I don't want him to call here." She looked at Mara almost sympathetically. "You be all right?"

"'s okay," muttered Mara evasively. "He's usually out anyway."

"Okay, you know now. I have to dress myself," she beamed. "We got tickets for quiz show on TV. Colleague of my husband. Knows someone there. Will be fun for sure."

Mara managed to produce a smile.

"If the baby cry," said Mrs. Vrabec, "is not bad, boy don't wake up properly. Babies often cry in sleep."

30

SUDDENLY MARA'S EXCITEMENT FELL away. Her mother had phoned, but she'd called a neighbor, not her.

Now that she knew her mother was more or less okay and that she hadn't totally forgotten her, she suddenly didn't feel much relief anymore. The feeling of breathing out gave way to something else.

She was her daughter and she was alone. Why hadn't her mother tried to get in touch with her? Why hadn't it occurred to her mother that she might be worried?

Why had she called Mrs. Vrabec? What on earth was that about? And then she knew. She hasn't got the guts, she thought, to explain to me why she's taken off. Hasn't got the guts! And she's not really interested in me, any more than my father is.

She remembered an incident.

She had been playing with her stuffed animals on the floor in the hall, she'd been nine or ten and she'd already realized that something wasn't right in this family. But she hadn't really known what it was. That day, she'd been round at her friend Dana's and had seen Dana's mother cuddle her and give her a kiss. On the way home, she'd seen a family out for a bicycle ride, and the father was mending the youngest son's bike, and they'd all stood around laughing. It had cut her to the quick. When she'd got home, her mother had been lying on the sofa watching TV. Mara had snuggled up to her, like a kitten seeking warmth.

"Move over, kid, I can't see the screen," her mother had said, pushing her away.

Mara had tried somehow to attract her attention, had let herself fall dramatically to the floor, her face in her hands. But her mother hadn't been looking.

She'd always wanted a pet when she'd been younger, a big, strong, gentle dog most of all, or even a cat wouldn't have been bad, something to fuss, something warm, living, that you could cuddle. Or a rabbit, a hamster. Anything. The only animal that she'd ever brought home and tried to hide had been a frog. But when her father had found it, he'd thrown it out the window.

I'll have to stop taking my family to heart so much, Mara thought. I can't let what happens here get to me. Every argument, every scene between her parents. She would have to be indifferent to them. What was it to her?

31

SHE GOT THE 5:10 P.M. bus toward the city. Mara sat by the window. The bus was almost empty. The sun was shining on her face, hurting her eyes. She stood up and sat with her back to the driver.

The streets were full of people, as if everyone had ventured out of their holes at once to enjoy the summer evening after yesterday's rain. Flowers in concrete tubs shone as if they'd just been washed. The sky was spotlessly blue.

Mara looked out and wondered what day it was. Wednesday? Or Thursday? What on earth was the date? She had lost all sense of time. She felt like an astronaut floating through space after losing the connection to his ship.

People got on the bus and off again, one person laughed, someone else was talking to his child, someone was babbling into a cell phone. She didn't listen, the people had nothing to do with her. Someone tripped over her feet. When the bus went round a corner, a woman, who was just trying to get past her, lost her balance and fell on top of her. Mara absent-mindedly put out her arm to catch her and the woman thanked her. Mara smiled and carried on staring out of the window.

And started.

Tim! She saw him and sat bolt upright.

There was Tim!

He was riding next to them on his scooter! Without a helmet! And on the seat behind him was a girl in a summer dress, with blond hair and a red velvet hair band. She was snuggling right up to the boy, her legs shone white in the sun. She had her arms around Tim and her head against his back, a broad grin on her face. She was wearing white sandals and had polished toenails.

Mara could see it all clearly because Tim was riding right next to her. She rubbed her eyes. What was this? What was going on here? Tim was riding his scooter between the bus and the pavement with a blond girl in a flowery dress and a red hairband. Blond, straight hair, shoulder length, fluttering in the wind. Tim had his head thrown back and he beamed. She could see his white teeth, his lips, see him squinting because the sun was dazzling him.

He had no idea that she was so close to him, next to him, only separated from her by the wall of the bus. He didn't have a clue.

Sometimes, when Mara watched a film on TV that didn't go the way she expected, she just flicked to a different channel. She felt like that now. This picture had to be wiped away, replaced by another one: flick! And suddenly this bus, in which she was sitting, wouldn't be driving through the city but along the banks of a lake, sailing boats on glittering water, old tall trees, casting shadows, snow-capped mountains on the horizon . . . Yes, that was it, Tim and this blonde must be a mirage that could dissolve, be carried away by the wind, gone, never seen.

Or was it reality?

That Tim—her Tim—was giving a lift to a girl down there? Laughing? Looking happy?

How could you bear to believe that you'd really seen something like that?

Why was she still breathing in and out and in and out?

Why was she sitting there, quite calmly, not on the rampage? Or shouting? Or smashing the bus to smithereens?

Why was she so calm?

And just watching what was going on down there, next to her on the street?

Why hadn't she lost it?

Her head was a big, shapeless, boiling balloon, this monstrous hammering thing sitting on her shoulders. Her feet were ice-cold however; she could hardly feel them. But there was this prickling sensation in her legs, as if armies of ants were running all over them. Like sometimes when she woke up at night because the arm she'd been lying on had gone to sleep. But worse. Much worse.

She wished she could take her body off, like a pair of jeans. Drop it and step away from it into another life.

That girl there and him—they seemed so intimate. It was unbelievable. They were a couple and riding next to Mara as if to annoy her, as if to show her how good life could be, how wonderful, how happy, how easy . . . And now, as if the girl could read Mara's mind or as if she felt her gaze, she looked up, directly through the bus window, at Mara. She had blue eyes. And freckles on her nose. Her lips were smeared with lipgloss and shone. She had little studs with colored stones in her ears. She was so close that Mara almost could have touched her, if it hadn't been for the thick pane of glass between them. She looked about fifteen.

Was it French club again? Or wasn't there supposed to be some stupid furniture delivery today? What excuses would he make when she confronted him? And expect her to swallow them!

Mara got more and more furious. She couldn't take her eyes off the girl. She noted every detail about her, and everything she saw made her want to puke. Made her so angry that she'd have liked to break the window, to grab the girl, pull her off that scooter with one snatch, like a sci-fi film, like Lara Croft would have done.

That was the sort of girl that boys swarmed around. The sort who could have her pick of the guys, who'd always find someone willing, a slave to do everything for her, to drive her anywhere, pick her up from anywhere, send her love letters. That was the sort of girl who never got dumped . . . The lousy little blond tart, she looked like someone Mara would love to beat up. Beat to a pulp. Knock her out . . . How could she have believed for a second that Tim was different from the boys she knew? Somehow better. That it would be worth wasting more than a thought on him.

At the intersection, the light changed to amber and the bus braked. But Tim accelerated and the scooter purred across the junction at the last second. Mara could still see the girl's summer dress, still see the bright hair fluttering in the wind, and she felt as if she could hear their laughter. Their happiness.

She stuffed her fists into her mouth, biting on the soft flesh until it bled. And the pain numbed her for a second. And she knew: she couldn't go to her mother, not now, not today. Not after she'd seen Tim and that girl.

She couldn't help her mother, she'd have to see how she managed with her own life, how she dealt with this chaos.

32

HER FATHER WAS AT home. He was sitting on the sofa, scratching a mosquito bite on his forearm and watching baseball.

"Sit down, girl," he said as she stood in the doorway. "These bastards don't stand a chance against my boys."

Mara watched for a moment from a distance as an outfielder pounced on a loose ball—which was really good. But after that bus journey just now, after Tim and the blonde on his scooter, she wasn't in the mood for anything, let alone baseball.

Her father slapped his thighs. "See that!" he shouted. "Did you see that?"

"I met Droste," said Mara. Her father jumped and glanced sideways at her. "And?" he asked.

"He wants money. It's getting serious," answered Mara. "I don't want to pay for this. Can't you get something to him at least?"

"What do you mean pay for it?" her father suddenly pricked up his ears. "What does he want from you?"

"What do you think?" said Mara.

Her father stared at her. His eyes were glassy, but he wasn't completely drunk yet.

"The pig!" he swore furiously. "If I catch him!"

"Calm down, nothing happened. I can look after myself."

"Fair enough!" Her father nodded and took another swig from his can.

Mara watched him. It's lovely how you care for me, she thought. Just lovely.

The living room got messier every day. Mara kept her own room, the kitchen, and the bathroom tidy, as well as she could. But he never cleaned anything up, not the softened pizza cartons, not the thin, used paper napkins. He didn't put the ketchup bottle back in the fridge. At the moment, it was under the table in front of the sofa. She wondered whether she should clean up in here, but all things considered, it would be a waste of effort.

"Heard anything from your mother?" her father called when she was already back out in the hall.

"No!" yelled Mara. She went to the hall cupboard, removed the paper with her mother's address, which Mrs. Vrabec had given her, from her jacket pocket, went to her bedroom, and put it face down in her desk drawer.

She had other things to worry about.

Tim and his girlfriend were probably riding along by the lake, and perhaps they'd stopped at the café where she'd been with Tim, which would be open today, of course. Bright sun umbrellas, happy people, the clatter of glasses and cutlery. And he'd buy her a Coke or something and make eyes at her. Thoughts are free. Is there punk in your soul?

It had all been garbage. French club, yeah right! How stupid must his mother be?

In her room, she threw herself onto the bed. It smelled musty. She stood up again and opened the window.

It was seven o'clock: the sound of the news announcer's "good evening" floated up from the apartment below; the children who'd been playing in the street had gone home.

A man was down on the street, washing his car with a large, soft sponge, as tender as if it were his wife's back. Mara watched for a while.

Then she turned away, took off her sneakers, her socks, her pants, her T-shirt, threw it all on the floor and threw herself on the bed again. The twittering of the birds came through the window. They became active again around now, before night fell.

There was a car taking forever to start. It spluttered and popped and some of the stench seemed to find its way up here. Mara lay on her back, her arms behind her head, watching a cloud slowly dispersing outside the window, high in the sky. She suddenly found herself thinking about Mrs. Sidler. She must know by now.

It occurred to her that maybe the right thing to have done would be to phone Mrs. Sidler, to tell her herself, to explain why she had ... Katie ...

I'll go into the school tomorrow, thought Mara before she fell asleep. I'll talk to her. I've got to do it.

But that wasn't the way it turned out.

33

THE NEXT MORNING SHE woke up thinking of Tim.
They were painful thoughts. For a moment the blood
hammered in her head.

Should she try to phone him again? See what he had to
say for himself?

Her father was in the bathroom. The telephone was lying
on the floor, next to the full ashtray. Mara emptied the ashtray and took the phone into the kitchen.

Her father must have done some shopping yesterday.
There was half a bag of peeled potatoes, a bag of white onions,
baloney, cheese, a loaf of bread, eggs, margarine, and beer.

At some point last night he'd made fried potatoes. The
pots and pans were still lying around.

She stared at the telephone. It was almost nine. Tim
might have first period free. Perhaps he hadn't left his cell
phone at home for once . . .

She dialed his number.

She imagined Tim and a group of guys wandering around
the school grounds, the girl casting melting looks at him,

which he acknowledged with a cool smile. She had been to the Bolivar School once, with her class, to see an African dance group. Mrs. Sidler had organized it. The school had a hall, like a proper theater, with raised tiers of seats and an orchestra pit.

The school also had a garden, which was split into vegetable and flower plots that were looked after by various groups. There was also a terrarium and an aquarium. When she had asked why they didn't have cool stuff like that at Brentwood School, Mrs. Sidler had explained that the parents got involved with that kind of thing at this school, that they donated money and so on. Then Mara hadn't asked any more questions. Because her parents obviously wouldn't donate a single lousy dollar for anything.

The voicemail cut in. So either Tim had left his cell phone behind again, or it wasn't a break, or he didn't want to answer it, because he was in the middle of making out with the poisonous blonde.

Suddenly she knew what she'd do. She pushed aside the thought of going into school to see Mrs. Sidler. Her discussion about the day-care center would have to wait.

She had to see Tim—that was all that mattered now. She had to hear what he had to say.

She got off the bus at an intersection. She could have caught another bus there and got off directly outside Tim's school, but she'd rather run. She hadn't run enough in the last few days, she could feel it.

She warmed up. She found her rhythm and increased the pace. She ran along the edge of the four-lane road. The pavement was wide, but there were all those empty patches for the newly planted trees, and you could easily lose your stride when you had to go around them. Once, Mara had been coming along here in early spring when a couple of trucks had been delivering the new trees and the municipal gardeners in their overalls had been shoveling earth. The trees had all taken root well; there was fresh growth on all the branches now.

The Bolivar School was being replastered and scaffolding was everywhere: a complicated structure of iron bars, hinges, and platforms. There were tarpaulins over the windows on the first floor, and there were big signs over the main entrance to the site explaining the building works.

Mara walked into the grounds through the open gate. She looked up at the building's facade but had no idea what classroom Tim would be in. She looked at her watch. It was nearly ten.

She wandered slowly around the large old building, past bike racks, the entrance to the cellar, the outbuildings, Latin mottoes over all the doors. One class seemed to be having an art lesson, as she could see several students out on the grounds with drawing tools.

Two boys were sitting under a tall tree and sketching the front of the main building. A girl was crouched in front of one of the old, baroque wooden doors with a pad of paper, holding her pencil against the light like a measuring stick and squinting. Mara walked closer and glanced at the paper. The girl looked up and smiled. "It's pretty difficult," she said shyly.

Mara shrugged and walked on. The caretaker was rolling a trash can over the yard; he didn't take any notice of her. There were a few benches in front of the high fence that separated the sports fields from the school grounds, with a group of boys sitting on them, also with drawing blocks. Mara guessed they were drawing the wire netting of the fence.

Nobody took any notice of her as she explored. She was killing time, the bell would have to go for a break sometime, then Tim would come down onto the school grounds, then she'd see... Up on the second floor, two teachers were standing by an open window chatting. The sound of a choir singing came from another window, and she heard a teacher scolding loudly... She heard the sparrows in the trees around the yard. She saw a car stopping outside on the street; someone was dropping off a latecomer, a small boy with a large backpack. She saw a girl with blond hair and a blue miniskirt walk across the school grounds. Her hair was smooth and reached to her shoulders.

Mara stopped, her heart thumped.

She saw the blond girl, carrying a drawing pad like the others, stop by the scaffolding and look at the construction thoughtfully. She was about fifteen and had hair clips holding her hair away from her face. Little colored stones glittered on her earlobes.

It was her! Tim's blonde.

So she was a student at the same school; of course, it all made sense. And of course she was wearing lipgloss again. Mara stood as if she'd been turned to stone.

The blonde had on an expensive-looking jacket over a blouse that must have cost loads too, like her skirt, her bag, and her shoes.

She had her cell with her. It rang.

Mara watched as the girl dug around in her bag, fished out a cell phone, gleaming silver and almost as small as a matchbox, and flipped it open. She exclaimed something that Mara couldn't hear and walked a few steps farther along the building.

She must be talking to him. To Tim, it couldn't be anyone else.

Mara followed her.

If anyone had asked, What are you doing, why are you following this girl? she wouldn't have understood the question. She just had to! She couldn't do anything else but follow this girl, who drew Mara like a magnet. Mara absorbed everything she could see of her as if in a trance. The line of her hips, the tiny roll of fat over the top of her skirt, the glitter of her bracelet as she held the phone.

And the longer Mara looked, the more details she took in, the hotter she got. And her heart beat frantically.

She could have launched herself on the girl like a lioness. She could have done it.

But she was still in control. It couldn't be here, she thought, shaking, not on the school grounds. Too many people. I must leave her alone here. But perhaps she'll walk farther, somewhere where I'm alone with her... perhaps then... something'll... happen...

Suddenly the girl tossed her head back and laughed, and

for a second, her blond hair looked like flowing golden water, and Mara struggled to breathe.

Tim can't even be here today after all, he couldn't talk to her during classes. He's telling her that he loves her, that she's so beautiful it makes his head ache, that he can't survive a second without her, that he wants to see her bare legs on his scooter, that he wants to feel her arm around his stomach again and her breasts against his back.

The blond girl wandered unsuspectingly on, the cell in her hand, and rounded the corner of the building. Now she was out of sight of the others in her drawing class. She was standing in front of the scaffolding and concentrating on what she was listening to, her whole face shining with joy. And happiness.

Then Mara leapt on her from behind. Soundlessly, with all her weight. And hit her with all her strength.

The cell flew in a wide arc through the air as the girl crashed into the iron bars and slumped to the ground. Without making a sound.

Nobody had seen anything. Suddenly the sparrows in the trees were quiet. Mara wanted to run away, but there was something stopping her, she couldn't move. She stared at the girl who'd been so beautiful just a moment ago but who was now lying there like a floppy rag doll. She saw blood slowly trickling from a wound on her temple and flowing into her hair. The girl was still.

Suddenly Mara was panic-stricken.

What if she's dead! the thought flashed through her head.

Then I'm a . . . murderer?

She bent down, slowly, as if under immense strain, turned the girl's shoulder, looked into her face. The girl looked back with empty eyes, like a blind person.

"Can you... can you hear me?" whispered Mara. She looked around. It was quiet; nobody in sight. The girl twitched her eyelids and opened her mouth but nothing came out except a deep, painful groan.

Mara let go of the girl's shoulder and stood up.

The girl was alive.

She stood next to the motionless body like a hunter next to his prey. She didn't know what to do now. She had done what she'd wanted desperately to do, but now she felt nausea rise up in her.

What had happened? She'd had a fight, like so often, had beaten someone up like so often, but it had never been like this, from an ambush. Or so violent.

She took a deep breath, looked up to the sky, and fixed her gaze on the girl on the ground in front of her again. She wasn't moving.

Someone should call a doctor, she thought.

She looked around again. She didn't know where the exit was anymore, the school gate. She didn't know why she was here anymore. Her head was spinning.

I must do something, she thought. I must do something! But nothing came to her.

It was as if her mind had given up, as if her head was refusing to have anything more to do with her.

She needed to get off the grounds by the quickest route, without being seen. Her mind was working that much. She couldn't go back past the students with their drawing pads. She'd have to go around the building, in the other direction, away from here.

Suddenly, the girl in front of her whimpered. A high, plaintive tone that ignited Mara's brain like a burning match.

She ran.

And stopped, slowed down, went back to her strolling pace. She mustn't look suspicious, whatever happened.

As she came around the next corner, she saw a teacher. He was standing with two boys in the middle of the gravel path that led around the school and they were all looking at the gables, pencils in hand. Mara wanted to avoid them, walk around them on the grass, in a wide circle.

Then she heard the cry. It was a boy shouting, his voice full of panic, high-pitched. "Help! Over here!"

At the same moment, the teacher turned in her direction and looked at her.

Mara said hello. She had the presence of mind to listen to the cries for help before turning and running back, as if following the cries.

Then she heard a second voice: "Help! Quickly! Where is everybody?"

She saw the open basement window, a dark hole in the brickwork. She jumped blindly and landed hard on the concrete floor.

The light in here was dim. She blinked. The cellar was empty except for the shelves along the walls. There was old equipment on the shelves, bottles and microscopes for chemistry and physics. And files. Full of yellowing sheets.

She waited until her eyes became used to the light. The door was in the wall opposite the window. She carefully pushed the handle. It was locked. She was trapped!

Mara leaned against the cracked wood of the door, breathing heavily. She heard hurried steps outside the window, heard people calling.

"A doctor, quickly!"

"Of course I know the emergency number!"

"We must take her into the office!"

"Who could have done this?"

She slowly slid down the door until she was crouching. She pressed her arms to her chest. Time passed. Then more steps. A deeper voice, a teacher.

"What's keeping the police? When is the ambulance coming?"

Someone joined them, a woman.

"Will she survive?"

Then the steps faded away.

It was completely silent for an eternity. Until the blare of the ambulance sirens. They approached at amazing speed. Mara could hear more excited shouts and then tires scrunching over the gravel.

Someone shouted orders. "To the right! Here! Watch out for the corner!"

And always the sirens. A deafening noise that almost split Mara's head.

Then the school bell rang. A little later, the usual sound of hundreds of students clattering through the building, out onto the school grounds. Then there was a sudden noisy hush, as if everyone outside was holding their breath, along with a whispering, a mumbling from hundreds of mouths. And quietly, a few students right outside the window: "Is she dead?"

"Do you know what happened? Get out of the way there! The ambulance needs to get through!"

"Have you heard? A girl in grade 9!"

Then nobody passed for a while.

Mara crouched on the damp concrete floor and stared wide-eyed at the bright rectangle of the window. It seemed unattainable. She had no idea how to get out of here again. But she'd have to try. She stood and limbered up her muscles. She fixed her eyes on the metal window frame and jumped. Her hands grabbed at nothing. She couldn't do it, the window was too high.

She tried a second time and failed again. The third time she managed to grab the frame, but at that moment the sirens sounded again and the ambulance raced past. Only a few inches away, out on the gravel. Students followed the vehicle, running after it toward the gate.

She couldn't hold on any longer and fell to the ground so hard she winded herself. She twisted on the floor, panting in desperation. Endless seconds went by before the air poured into her lungs again. She groaned loudly.

She sat there for several minutes, her eyes shut, breathing.

The bell went for the next class. There was the sound of trampling feet again through the corridors and hallways above her, voices again. Doors banged. Then it was quiet. As if the school was holding its breath.

Mara pulled a few files off the shelves and stacked them up against the wall under the window. She climbed onto the wobbly tower and gripped the window frame. Clenching her teeth, she pulled herself up. Pushed her head out. She saw the bushes, the lawn, the gravel path. There was nobody to be seen. She forced herself through the window opening, stood up, brushed the dirt off her clothes, and slunk, ducking along the wall, around the side to the front, where she ran to the school entrance. From there she walked tall and deliberately to the main gate. It was probably fifty yards, but it felt never-ending. The school windows were at her back, somebody could be standing at any of them, watching her. Noticing her. She just had to keep walking slowly; she mustn't draw attention to herself.

She walked through the gate. At the edge of the road to her left was a police car. It was empty. She turned right. A bus passed her. She saw the bus stop and now she began to run. She saw the bus pull up to the stop and brake, saw the doors open, a couple of kids jump out onto the pavement. Three boys, maybe eleven or twelve. She ran faster, she raised her arm and hoped the driver could see her in his side mirror.

The driver waited until she'd jumped on at the back doors and signaled to him. He waved back in a leisurely way and the doors closed.

She took a deep breath. She didn't know where it came from, but for a fraction of a second, she felt a particular sensitivity for time and space, an impression of something, a "system" that raised up all of humankind in total confidence that everyone who used it was good. And hadn't just hospitalized somebody else.

She didn't even dare to sit down. The driver was watching her in his rearview mirror.

"Have you got a bus pass?" he called.

"Yes, of course," said Mara, struggling to keep her voice level while she pulled out her pass.

"Okay then," said the driver, pulling away.

She hoped that the girl on the school grounds hadn't really been seriously injured. She hoped it so fervently that she believed it.

The bus gradually emptied, and Mara got off at the intersection and took the next bus back. They crossed two bridges; twice she looked down at the river, at barges laden with supplies and willows trailing their branches in the water. They drove through an industrial area, and Mara got off when she saw a hot-dog stand with sun umbrellas and old beer barrels covered with circles of chipboard. Men were standing around the barrels drinking.

She bought a Coke and a hot dog and perched on the curb a little distance away. She knew that the men were looking at her, and she heard one of them call out to her that she was welcome to join them, they weren't chauvinist pigs. And she heard them all laughing.

She stuffed the rest of the hot dog in her mouth and threw the garbage in the Dumpster.

She ran away from there. Aimlessly. This way and that. Eventually she arrived at the commuter station, just as the sun was setting. There was a red glow in the sky, reflected in the windows of the travel information center. Mara saw a little line of travelers waiting at the only open window. A punk with a pit bull and half a ton of metal chains around his stomach was wandering up and down outside the center. He had a Mohawk. Mara watched him for a while, wondering whether she should speak to him. Ask for a cigarette or something, not that she wanted one: she didn't smoke.

But she wanted to hear a human voice saying something to her. Didn't matter what, anything.

She'd been out for almost ten hours now, and her legs were tired and her head was empty.

Somewhere, in another part of town, a girl with blond hair was lying in a hospital bed, cared for by the doctors and her family. And the telephone was ringing in one of the nice houses on Cudworth, where Tim lived, and someone was saying, "Your girlfriend was beaten up."

The pit bull came over to her, sniffed at her, and wagged its tail. It opened its wide mouth and panted, its slimy pink tongue slipping back and forth, creating a froth of drool. It looked gruesome, with protruding eyes and a neck rippling with muscle. But Mara bent down and patted the beast all the same. She wasn't afraid that the dog would bite her, although it had teeth like a shark.

She wasn't afraid because she didn't care what happened to her.

The punk nodded to her and whistled to his dog. They went in opposite directions.

Under some trees, Mara found a bench that hadn't yet been occupied by a homeless guy. She lay down on it and covered herself with her jacket.

There were loads of birds in the trees, some of them made cawing noises. She opened her eyes wide each time and stared into the nighttime darkness of the leaves but couldn't make anything out.

When she nodded off briefly, she dreamt about a hospital, where doctors were bending over an injured girl. Doctors with facemasks and little glasses, like magnifying glasses. They were busy with forceps and scalpels and talking during the operation. "It's critical," one said.

And Mara walked through walls and could step through closed doors. She came across Tim, sitting on a folding chair by a white wall. "What have you done?" he asked. Then she woke up with a shiver. She got up from the bench and walked a few paces until the blood began to pulse through her body again.

She thought about her parents. About Simone. She thought of the life that she'd led, the family that she'd been born into. You can't choose your family, someone had said once.

It was true. And her family hadn't been able to choose her either.

A girl who couldn't control her anger, a girl who couldn't deal with her rage. A girl who hit out before she thought.

That's what they always said about thugs, that they used their fists because their heads were full of straw. But she, Mara, could use her head too. Had more than just straw.

She thought about her grandparents and an orchard where bright autumn leaves were falling, and about those leaves covering everything, the lawn, the flowerbeds, the old stone steps, the table and the garden chairs, and she heard mournful music that made her cry suddenly.

She saw a child in the orchard, with a red cap and a woolen scarf wrapped twice round her neck, running around in the rustling leaves, kicking up the leaves with her little boots and squealing with joy.

She remembered once, when she'd been very small, waking up in the middle of the night. Her mother was lying next to her and holding her in her arms, really close, and whispering something quietly. The next morning her mother was the same as usual, and at first Mara hadn't been sure whether she'd only dreamt it. But she'd felt happy for days.

34

WHEN DAWN BROKE, MARA went back to the station, washed her face in the washroom, held her hands under the drier, and, as a cleaning woman grumpily wiped down one of the cubicles, sneaked a few coins from the woman's cart.

She stopped by the station bakery. Should she have croissants? Or a Chelsea bun?

As she wondered what her stomach fancied, she felt sick.

She ran back to the washroom, dropped the coins on the cart, and leaned over the sink.

"Problems, dear?" asked the cleaning woman, putting her heavy hand on her back. "Need anything?"

Mara rinsed her mouth, spat out the water, and raised her head. She looked at the woman. An old, worn-out, weary face.

She thought, I wonder what sort of life she's had, what sort of childhood, what sort of parents, what sort of husband.

She smiled and shook her head. "Thanks," she said, "I'm okay."

As she left the station, she suddenly knew what to do.

35

MARA CROUCHED ON THE steps outside the detached house where Mrs. Sidler lived with her husband. It was a small house with a pointed roof, red brickwork, white windows, and flowers in the front garden. The laburnum was in bloom.

There was a newspaper and a fat brown envelope in the mailbox by the white front door.

It was Saturday. Mara knew that her teacher would be at the school this morning, as once a month she held a consultation for parents who worked. But Mara felt that she couldn't speak to her there. She'd go to her home. She knew the address. Mrs. Sidler had written it on the board once and said that if they ever had any problems, they could come to her at any time for help and advice. She was the only person at the school who'd do anything like that, give out her home telephone number, her home address. Mara had never taken her up on it.

But now the moment had come. She didn't know where else to go. She was desperate. She needed somebody to help her, to stand by her in what she intended to do.

Mrs. Sidler came home just before three-thirty. She pushed her bicycle, which was loaded down with bulging carrier bags, through the garden gate. Her hefty school bag was on the luggage carrier, probably full of test papers.

Mara got up slowly. She was almost stiff. She felt like a puppet that needed someone to pull the strings, first the right leg, then the left, straighten the back, head up.

"You!" Mrs Sidler looked at her. She narrowed her eyes to little slits.

Everything about her was defensive and rejecting. Of course, she must think that Mara was here about the problem at the day-care center. No wonder she didn't want anything to do with her.

Mara greeted her quietly.

"Hello."

The teacher leaned her bicycle silently against the wall, pulled the bags from the handlebars and put them on the ground. Then she went over to Mara. "What do you want? We've got nothing more to say to each other. What you did at the day-care was unforgivable."

Mara couldn't reply. She opened her mouth, took a breath, shook her head. Then she finally got out, "But it's not . . . not about that. It's much . . . much worse." She turned away.

"Okay then, come in." Mrs. Sidler had become pensive. "Can you give me a hand with the bags?"

Mara wanted to say, Of course I can, but again she couldn't get the words out. She felt sick, she was dizzy, the world seemed to be spinning around her. Very carefully, with one of the full carrier bags in each hand, she followed the teacher, waited until she'd unlocked the door and, groaning slightly, put her heavy school bag down on the floor. Mrs. Sidler nodded toward a door on the right. "That's the kitchen," she said. "It all goes in there."

Mara entered a bright, tidy room; the pans were hanging over the stove, next to a drying rack and a magnetic strip with the kitchen knives stuck all in a row. Below the window was a fruit bowl. Apples, black plums, a pear with little brown spots. Clean dishes in the drying rack. Everything was like a film set. Real kitchens didn't look like this.

All of a sudden, something soft and gentle rubbed against her legs. When she looked down, she saw a black cat with its tail in the air circling her and purring.

"That's Merlin, my fat old tomcat," the teacher said.

Mara didn't answer. She raised her head. Mrs. Sidler was setting the bags down on the table and watching her. She waited.

Mara's hands were shaking so badly she hid her arms behind her back.

How should she tell her? She had spent the whole day thinking like mad since she'd known, since she'd realized that she couldn't go on like this. Should she tell her the whole story at once? Everything that had gone through her head last night and the last few days? How she often felt like a little kid, how sad she often was, without knowing why? What she was like inside when she felt this unbridled hot rage, when the red mist rose up unstoppably before her eyes and her skull threatened to burst? And what was going on at home, her parents' constant fighting, her father's violence, that her mother had just up and left, left her alone?

Should she tell her teacher all that first? Before she got to the awful bit, to what had happened yesterday, what she'd done, that it had been her who'd injured a girl so badly?

She didn't know how to, here in this spotlessly clean, tidy kitchen. She didn't know where to start. And so she started with the sentence that should have been the end of her story.

"I wanted to ask you if you . . . if you could take me to a home."

Mrs. Sidler froze. There was a long moment of silence. Then she repeated, "To a home?"

Mara nodded. Her eyes filled with tears.

"What sort of a home? And why do you want . . . ?"

Mara couldn't say anything else. She suddenly sobbed.

Mrs. Sidler moved, picked up the kitchen stool and sat down, her hands between her knees. She looked firmly at Mara.

"Why do you want that?" she asked calmly.

Mara felt as if she could just collapse at any moment; everything was spinning around her. The carousel of her thoughts was whirling behind her forehead, getting faster and faster all the time.

"Mara, what's happened?" Her teacher's voice reached her, hardly audible, very gentle.

Mara opened her mouth; her lips were like sandpaper, so dry. She shook her head and shrugged helplessly.

She cleared her throat several times and wiped her eyes.

And then she said it, so quietly that she could hardly hear her own voice: "I've really messed up. A girl from the Bolivar School, I...I don't know. It's...I didn't mean to...I don't even know..."

Mrs. Sidler raised her head. Red spots had suddenly appeared on her cheeks. Of course she'd heard about it. "That was you?" she whispered.

Mara heard the fear in her whisper. The fear that her teacher had for her, for her life, for her future. For everything. She heard the fear that sounded like sympathy, like a kind of love that she had for her, and then she could no longer hold it in. She burst into silent tears and flung her arms around her teacher's neck.

Mrs. Sidler held her tight, said nothing, waited, was just there for her. And then at last Mara spoke, haltingly, in fragments, all over the place and confused. First of all about Katie and the nursery, and all that, then about her mother, who'd vanished and finally called, about Tim, how she'd liked him, and the girl on the scooter. And that she'd wanted to talk to Tim, that nothing would have happened if fate hadn't crossed their paths when she was on the bus, if fate hadn't led her straight to that girl, of all people, standing next to the scaffolding—

"Did you fight? What did you do to her?"

"I...attacked her. She didn't know..." said Mara. "I don't know how badly she's injured, but"—she broke off, looked up at her teacher— "it must be bad. She's in pain."

"How do you know that?"

"I can feel it."

"That's your guilty conscience talking to you," said Mrs. Sidler. Her voice was louder now.

Mara nodded.

"You need someone to take the guilty conscience away for you, but I can't do that, you know that." She pressed her lips together, was silent for a moment, then said, "There's no excuse for what you've done. There may be an explanation, but you've probably discovered that for yourself by now."

Mara remained silent, although she knew that Mrs. Sidler was waiting for an answer. But what else could she say? She had said everything. She had said that she needed to go somewhere to get help, where they'd protect her from herself.

When Mara continued to say nothing, Mrs. Sidler suddenly stretched out her hand and said, "Come on, let's go."

"Where?" asked Mara.

"To the police. I want you to repeat everything you've just told me. To turn yourself in. That's what I want. To go there together and to hear you say, I've done something wrong. I deserve to be punished. Do you understand? And then, I promise, I'll find you a place in a home. But we've got to go to the police first. You are totally responsible for your actions. Nobody else. Not your father. Not your mother. Not the school. Just you and you alone. As a citizen, as a member of society. That's the most important thing for you to understand. We'll go to the police and you'll tell them that you're prepared to accept the punishment for your actions."

Mrs. Sidler looked at her steadily. "You'll have to learn to control yourself, your feelings, your aggression. I want to help you do that."

36

THE POLICE HEADQUARTERS WAS an imposing building with a courtyard separating the prison cells from the police station. The patrol cars were parked in the courtyard along with police vans, with barred windows, which could perhaps be used to transport prisoners as well.

As they'd walked down the long hallway on the first floor, Mara had been able to catch a glimpse of the prison opposite through the windows, which sent a shiver down her spine. All the windows were square and the same size, three storys high. Some had towels fluttering from them.

Mrs. Sidler had been very tense all the way to headquarters, had held tight to Mara's arm as if she'd been afraid that she'd run away at the last minute.

Now they were sitting in a narrow yellow room, facing the street, and the noise of the rush-hour traffic sounded through the open window.

The police officer, Hubert Winkel—according to the nameplate on his desk—was sitting in front of mountains of files, next to photos of his wife and children, a vase of withered meadow flowers, and a plate holding an apple with a bite taken out of it.

The officer looked at Mara.

"It's a long time since any of you have come to give yourselves up when you've screwed up. You're usually proud of what you get up to."

Mrs. Sidler cleared her throat. "Not everyone's the same," she said severely. "Don't be so prejudiced."

The officer stared at the brown, half-eaten apple and threw it in the garbage.

The teacher had explained concisely to the officer what had happened and was waiting for him to ask Mara about it. But they'd been here twenty minutes now and the girl had hardly said a word. The officer more than made up for it. Since he'd found out that Mrs. Sidler was a teacher, he'd taken out all his frustration on her: over the violence in the schools, over what he called the absurd impression that the police were there to straighten out everything the parents and teachers had messed up in the kids, over the raids they'd had to make and the checkpoints they'd had to post outside every school to do that . . . and how the worst schools ought to be shut down altogether. Hubert Winkel talked and talked, and the more he talked, the more Mara wanted to get out of there. She didn't want to explain the things going on inside her to him. She couldn't even believe that she'd said to Mrs. Sidler, I want to go into a home.

But she was holding her hand.

"Mara spoke to one of your female colleagues a while ago,"

said Mrs. Sidler, glancing sideways at Mara. "What was her name? Can you remember?"

"Kinsey, or something," remembered Mara.

"Ah, Sabine Kinsey. Yes, she works here. She's on duty today. Why did you speak to her?"

"I just wanted to know where my mother was." The officer frowned.

"She knows now," said Mrs. Sidler insistently. "That's not why we're here."

"Constable Kinsey was nice." Mara nodded as if to confirm it.

"Ha." The officer leaned back. "So I'm not nice, is that it?"

Mara looked out the window. The teacher's grip tightened. "Sometimes it's easier for girls to talk to a woman," she said.

"Huh," muttered the officer. "Easier, who said anything about easier? I thought she wanted to turn herself in for beating someone up at the Bolivar School. And now she wants to put an end to it. That's what you said."

Mrs. Sidler nodded, Mara heard her sigh softly.

"Do you think I can't manage it? Enter the details into the computer? But by all means . . ." He stood up abruptly, pushed back his chair, and left the room. The door remained open. They saw uniformed police officers walking past; some of them looked in curiously. Mara sat as stiff as a poker and didn't move.

Next to her, Mrs. Sidler smiled encouragingly. "Just wait," she murmured, "we'll get there."

"I want to get out of here," answered Mara quietly. "This is no use."

"Do you want to give up again?" asked the teacher. "Is this all the patience you have for yourself?"

"It's nothing to do with patience," replied Mara. But she stayed put.

37

SHE WAS WEARING JEANS, a yellow-striped top, and cowboy boots. She smiled and stretched out her hand in greeting. She greeted the teacher first, then Mara.

"Hello," she said. "I'm Sabine Kinsey. I gather we've met before?" She looked at her in a friendly manner. No suspicion, just quite openly.

Mara could feel that things would go better with her. "We spoke on the phone," she answered, "a couple of days ago." Weird, only a couple of days. It felt more like a year. "About my mother." She gave her parents' names and the address. "The police were called by our neighbor..."

Sabine Kinsey exchanged glances with her colleague, Hubert Winkel, who was still standing in the doorway. "All yours," he said, gesturing invitingly at his computer. "I'll go and get myself a coffee." Turned round and shut the door behind him.

The constable sat down at the monitor. "Ah," she said after a while, "here we are. Yes. A Mrs. Vrabec called. She was afraid that something was going on in the apartment next door. It says here she said, 'He'll kill her, one day he'll kill her.'"

"Who does she mean?" asked Mrs. Sidler, as if she refused to understand.

"My father. Our neighbor meant that my father would kill my mother. But she's exaggerating. He wouldn't do that. Never."

Mara felt the two women's attentive glances. Kinsey turned back to the computer.

"Yes, and then you phoned. Did I know where your mother was, we chatted, and I said I would pass it on to my colleagues at social services. Which I did. Has anyone been around?"

Mara shook her head.

"No?"

"No."

"Okay, I'll take care of it. And now to the Bolivar School. And to you."

Kinsey looked seriously at Mara for a moment. She took the mouse, clicked on one thing after another, repeatedly shaking her head. Then she nodded.

"Ah, here's the report. Officers Beattie and Edwards. The call came from the Bolivar School around 10:12 a.m. At the same time as several calls from cell phones. From students. A girl was lying unconscious on the school grounds." She glanced at Mara. "That was her, right?"

She said nothing. Constable Kinsey kept reading, "There was evidence of violence used against her. She had a cut on her head and was unable to get up. Her legs ..." The officer's voice trailed off and then became clearer. "She was taken by ambulance to the Elizabeth Hospital. Probable injuries to the spinal column and a suspected fracture at the base of the skull."

Mrs. Sidler made a little shocked cry and put her hand over her mouth.

Mara crumpled up.

"The principal has said that he wants to press charges against an unknown assailant. On inquiring among the children who were on the school grounds at the time, it transpired that a girl"—Kinsey looked at Mara—"who was obviously not a member of the school, had been seen there at the time of the attack. That must have been you."

Mara's head began to burn up.

"In any case, questioning showed that the culprit was not thought to be a member of the Bolivar School."

"Mara attends Brentwood School," said Mrs. Sidler.

Constable Kinsey nodded. "Officers Beattie and Edwards then went to 12 Cudworth Way—"

Mara held her breath. "What? What did you say? But . . . that's Tim's address!"

"—to inform Sophie's parents," Kinsey continued. "Her name is—"

Mara felt as if she were suffocating. Her face flushed red. "What's her name?"

"Sophie Harris, aged fifteen," read the constable. "However, the officers only found the son, Tim Harris, aged seventeen, at home. He had not attended school that day because he had the flu. The parents only arrived later. They then drove straight to the hospital. There are no details here as to Sophie Harris's condition."

"What's the matter?" cried Mrs. Sidler.

She couldn't answer. She sat on her chair, her legs drawn up, her arms clinging to them, and silently hitting her head against her knees, over and over again. Hard. Each time a firework of pain exploded in her head. But she couldn't stop.

She thought, 12 Cudworth Way. Sophie Harris, sister of Tim, his sister! It was his sister on the scooter! It was his sister!

Two hands were laid on her shoulders, stroking her hair.

"Tell me what's wrong, Mara!" Mrs. Sidler cried out again. "Say something! Stop acting like that!"

How should I act? Mara wanted to ask. How should I act when I feel like scum? I can't think anymore, I don't want to think anymore.

I want to be dead, dead forever. Gone forever. I want . . .

Someone raised her head and something flowed into her mouth. A liquid.

"Swallow!" ordered the constable. And she swallowed. On autopilot. It made her eyes water because she imagined she'd swallowed something bitter, burning, acid or petrol, something dangerous. She swallowed. It was only water.

"Your teacher has already told me, but now I'm asking you, Mara Dolan." Constable Kinsey paused. "Was it you? You attacked that girl, this Sophie Harris, and left her lying there?"

Mara nodded.

"And you were shocked by what you'd done, and so you went to your teacher and told her?"

"She was in shock when she came to me," said Mrs Sidler. "And she had realized that she can't go on like this. I had hoped that that moment would come sooner. She could have spared herself and others a great deal."

"And," asked Kinsey, "what do you think will happen now?"

"I don't know," muttered Mara. "It's all too late anyway."

"It's never too late to turn around, never too late to change your life or your attitude to it," insisted Mrs. Sidler. "You know that. We've often spoken about it. I'm afraid you just never really listened. Believe me, it's never too late, Mara!"

It is! she thought. It's too late.

For a few seconds she saw Tim's face in her mind's eye, like a video clip. She saw his laugh, the nod of his head, the expansive gestures of his arms. And she remembered how he'd said her name and how he'd repeated her name. Mara. Her name had never sounded like it did when he said it. She shut her eyes.

Help me, she thought. Help me! Please!

I can't go on.

38

Dear Mr. and Mrs. Harris,

Allow me to introduce myself, my name is Suzanne Sidler and I am Mara Dolan's homeroom teacher. I believe I know her well—her good side as well as her bad side. She does have a good side. So I ask you to read a letter that Mara has written to you, which I enclose.

This letter is a break in Mara's life, a break between what happened in the past and what may come in the future.

As you know, the court case is proceeding and Mara knows that she is facing conviction. She welcomes this conviction. However, afterward she must have a chance for a new life—and you could help her in that if you were able to forgive her. Our society is based on a foundation of understanding, forgiveness, and pardon.

Mara got off to a bad start as a child. She was never taught any rules; nobody set her any boundaries. Mara now knows that a life without rules or boundaries leads to chaos; for her, it led to terrible aggression and acts of violence. She now has the deep desire to become a better person and to distance herself from this violence. She knows that she can learn to control her anger. She knows why she reacted in this way rather than another. And she condemns herself for it.

Therefore, I sincerely ask that you read Mara's letter. And, if you can find it in your hearts to do so, to send her a reply.

Please accept my very best wishes for your daughter, Sophie.

Yours sincerely,

Suzanne Sidler

Brentwood School

Dear Mr. and Mrs. Harris,

I would like to ask you to forgive me for what I did. I know that it is hard to forgive something so awful—I can't forgive myself. I ask myself all the time how I could have become such a monster, a girl that lots of people at school are afraid of, a girl who causes pain to innocent people.

Sometimes I wish that I'd dreamt it all and would soon wake up from this nightmare. But it was my real life. I didn't have any other life.

I know how hard it must be for you to read this letter and to accept that it was written by a girl who did something so bad to your daughter. Perhaps you can't even look at it.

When I got letters that I couldn't stand, I used to crumple them up and throw them away.

But perhaps you won't do that. I hope you won't. And I hope that you are more patient and know more about people.

I know that perhaps I can't really expect you to forgive me, but all the same, I'd like to try to apologize to you. And to tell you how I wish I could undo it all. How much I'd give for none of it to have happened.

I have been told that your daughter, Sophie, is still in hospital, that she has had very dangerous and complicated operations.

I think about your daughter all the time and about what she's going through and it seems so unfair that I'm not hurt, that I can walk.

I want to be punished for what I did. That's why I turned myself in.

There was such a huge anger in me for so long, so much rage against everything in my life, and I couldn't handle it.

I felt very unhappy in myself and I hit out around me, hurting innocent people.

That's what my life was like and I'm so ashamed.

They expelled me from school, I must accept that. There's no room there for someone like me. But my teacher, Mrs. Sidler, will still stand by me and I'm very grateful for that. I know that I can't expect it. And I will do everything I can not to disappoint her again. Mrs. Sidler always tried to convince me that violence isn't the way to deal with worries and fears, to solve conflicts. It's the opposite. It just makes everything worse.

I know it's hard for you to accept the apology of a girl who did something so dreadful to your daughter. But perhaps it might help you to know that things are bad for me, that I can't think about anything else, that what happened is really painful for me, so much that I often think I can't take anymore. I am eternally sorry, and I will never be able to be happy until Sophie is well again.

My teacher (who is letting me live with her at the moment) has found a place for me in a nearby girls' home for the duration of the court case.

She thinks that this home will be good for me because I can get psychological counseling there. I hope that I can go back there after the sentence. But that depends . . .

I promise that I will never give anyone else reason to be afraid of me. That I will never do anything to anyone else... I have a paper route in the mornings now. And after that I'm working in a laundry. All the money I earn is for Sophie. I would so like to do something for her.

Yours sincerely,
Mara Dolan

Hello, Mara,

We received your letter and we admit that it wasn't easy for us as parents, who live with Sophie's pain every day, to read it. Sophie will have to stay in the hospital for another four weeks and then she will go to a rehabilitation clinic for at least another six weeks. After that, according to the doctors, she might be able to lead a normal life, but that is still uncertain.

That's why we can't forget what you have done to us—and to our daughter above all. She was such a friendly girl who enjoyed life. Sophie never did anything to you. And even if she recovers, as we all hope she will—she will never forget what happened to her because of you. This has changed her life. It will be like a shadow over her for a long time to come. Our son has changed too, since the day his sister was injured like that. He has retreated into himself, he doesn't want to speak to anybody. He blames himself for falling for you. We try to talk him out of it, but it's difficult.

If you want to do something for Sophie, you could try to send her books. She reads a lot. Whether or not to accept them—she must decide that for herself.

It seems to us that you are very fortunate to have a teacher who cares for you and will stand by you. It is certainly best for you to be *in a home for the time being. And to begin the new life that your teacher talks of.*

You may write to us again and if you would like to say anything to Sophie, we will pass your letter on to her. She will have to open it herself though.

At the moment, Tim is not ready to speak to you. He needs time. And for Sophie to get better.

That is all we can do for you. The rest is in your hands. You have your life ahead of you. It is up to you to make something good with it from now on.

Peter and Sally Harris